THE *bad* KARMA DIARIES

Bridget Hourican

THE O'BRIEN PRESS
DUBLIN

First published 2011 by The O'Brien Press Ltd,
12 Terenure Road East, Rathgar, Dublin 6, Ireland.
Tel: +353 1 4923333; Fax: +353 1 4922777
E-mail: books@obrien.ie
Website: www.obrien.ie

ISBN:978-1-84717-085-9

1 2 3 4 5 6 7 8 9 10
11 12 13 14 15

The O'Brien Press receives
assistance from

Front cover image: iStockphoto
Editing, typesetting, layout and design: The O'Brien Press Ltd.
Printed by CPI Cox and Wyman Ltd
The paper used in this book is produced using pulp from managed forests.

DIARIES

BRIDGET HOURICAN has lived in a lot of cities beginning with 'B' – Belfast, Brussels, Budapest – but now lives in Dublin, where she rides her bike everywhere and writes articles for newspapers and magazines. She went to an international school in Brussels, which was a bit like the school in this book except with more languages. This is her first book for girls.

To Leanora

NEW YEAR'S DAY

Yesterday we dismantled our blog – or at least we cut it loose and sent it adrift into cyberspace, because apparently old blogs never die or disappear, they just circulate the web forever with nobody reading them (... that's making me think about infinity, which is making my head ACHE). Our blog was ... what was it? The public face of this diary? The diary's bad sister? Anyway, they were linked; I started them at (nearly) the same time and they were both really demanding. You can't write 'Did nothing today' in your diary 'cause it would make you feel like a boring person, and you DEFINITELY can't post that on your blog because your readers would be really unimpressed ... but keeping myself not-bored and my readers impressed is what made this term incredibly exciting, but also exhausting. If I hadn't had to keep feeding the diary and the blog, well, half the things that happened this term mightn't have happened ... I'm GLAD they happened, but now I want to step back a bit and let Karma settle!

O'Toole (our English teacher) says you have to know when to end – whatever it is you're writing, you should know when its moment is up. So sorry, diary, but your moment is up! It's the first of January and a new term will be starting soon, so now is the time to cut you loose ... yes, I KNOW you want to know what happened last night at Keith's party, but if I start writing entries again, well, soon I'll be caught in more adventures and there'll be no cut-off point. For

instance, last term I couldn't have stopped writing just when we set up the Instruments of Karma (to do nasty things to people who deserve it), or when I was fighting with Anna, or when I found out about Justine … because I was in the MIDDLE of all those things and I needed to see them through. You can't just stop writing about things when they're still going on. So since now we're on a break and nothing much is going on (except at Keith's party, when we … ha! No way!) …

It's goodbye (for now), diary, and you won't drift in cyberspace forever; you'll sit at the back of the drawer, and if you don't get thrown out, or lost, or burnt — yes, there's that risk, you're only paper! — then some day some lucky person will get to read all about Bomb and Demise and what happened when they set out on their marvellous adventures at the beginning of Second Year …

Denise Nelson (and Anna Power)

The Bad Karma Diaries

7 September–31 December

R.I.P.

MONDAY SEPTEMBER 7TH

Today is the first day of school, so here are my New Term Resolutions. Me and Anna (my best friend) don't do New Year Resolutions because what's called the New Year – 1 January – doesn't *feel* like the new year, it feels like the middle of the year. The *new* year is when you go back to school and you've moved up a year. So here are my New Term Resolutions:

* Study harder
* Eat healthy food
* Take up a sport
* Keep this diary
* Do some exciting stuff to put on our blog (mine and Anna's) – Urgent!!!
* Check out the new people in the class

I will explain about the blog tomorrow. I already started on the last resolution. The only interesting thing about the first day of term is the new people in your class. Because you never know – they might be the best fun, or they might be mad and crazy, or they just might fall in love with you. So anyway, we have a new boy and a new girl. The girl is called Heeun. She is from Korea and she looks stylish, or posh, or snobbish – not sure which! Well, she looks like when she's out of her uniform, she'll wear

very expensive clothes with designer labels. She is quite pretty. I think some of the boys are going to fancy her.

The new boy is called David Leydon. He has long hair and is very scruffy. Even though he is in a uniform same as everyone else he looks much scruffier. I don't think he talked to anyone all day. He looked fed-up and rebellious, but he's not exactly good-looking – he has spots – so it's hard to know if the girls are going to fancy him.

TUESDAY SEPTEMBER 8TH

Went to Anna's house after school. In her kitchen when we came in were her mum and Charlie (her baby brother) and then Tommy (her older brother) came in, and then Renata (her older sister) came in with Alva (a friend of Renata's). You can never predict who's going to be in Anna's, that's why it's exciting.

Once I said this to Anna and she said kind of sarcastically, 'Yeah, I know, what numbers are coming up today? It's like the Lotto.'

So now every time we reach her front door, I say, 'What are the Lotto numbers today?'

Her mum asked how was the diary coming on because the diary was her idea. She is a sighchiatrist (yes, I *know* this is not the right spelling, but it is Renata's joke; she says her mum's patients are always *sighing* about their problems). Anyway, being a psychiatrist (*there!*) makes Anna's mum very interested

in everything we're doing, I think.

When we were sitting round last week talking about what we were gonna put on our blog, she said, 'But if it's online, everyone can read it?' and we said, 'Well of *course*,' and then she said, 'But you need somewhere to confide your *private* thoughts.'

She said a diary was important for processing whatever was on our minds. As soon as she said 'processing', Renata snorted and shot up from her book, '*Processing?* You want to turn their thoughts into Easi Singles?'

Her mum said, 'Oh, Renata!'

Anna and I exchanged a look. In Anna's kitchen Renata is always reading a book and making like she's not listening but then she'll suddenly shoot into the conversation with some remark that you can't (well *I* can't) understand. And her mum always says, 'Oh, Renata!' in a warning voice, but also in a kind of delighted voice. You can tell she thinks the remark is brilliant, really. Me and Anna call it Renata's Snort, Swivel, Swat routine. It goes like this

1. *Snort*

2. Look up from book

3. *Swivel* eyes in our direction

4. Nasty/incomprehensible remark (that's the *Swat* – she swats us like flies)

5. 'Oh, Renata!'

6. Back down to book

They didn't ask me to stay for dinner so I had to come home. Fishfingers and chips and peas. Boring! Unhealthy! At Anna's they were having Rat-a-too-ee. At least that is what it sounds like. Exciting! Probably healthy! It is going to be easier for Anna to keep her New Term Resolution to eat healthy food than it is for me. I told my mum about my resolution and that she needed to help by not serving fishfingers and chips (peas are okay).

She said, 'Well, make your own then!' in a snappy way.

I noticed that Justine (my younger sister) was not really eating her chips either. Maybe we will go on strike together against Mum's unhealthy cooking!

WEDNESDAY SEPTEMBER 9TH

Just got text from Anna:

demise, don't forget rules for oaths

That was easy, so I texted right back:

Thanks, bomb, in the bag, how's trials?

Response:

Inside on vast, feel eat and pick, on brain, can't study...

Whaaaatttt ...? Couldn't work *that* one out. Had to unscramble. Then I texted back:

Greedy any!

This is in our top secret texting language! What we actually wrote is:

Denise, don't forget ruler for maths

Thanks, Anna, in the bag, how's tricks?

Gorged on tart, feel fat and sick, no brain, can't study...

Greedy cow!

OK, so our top-secret texting language is not so hard to work out ... Clue: our names, Denise and Anna, come out as 'Demise' and 'Bomb'. In fact our names coming out like that is what got us started because they don't just sound funny, they belong together, because bombs cause demises.

Anna always says, 'When I explode, you die, so I'm the boss of you!'

The rule is you have to use the first word that predictive texting throws up. This means we're always looking for odd words, because normal words like 'thanks' and 'can't' and 'feel' just come up as themselves. Of course Anna wouldn't normally write 'gorged on tart', she'd write 'ate too much cake', but that wouldn't come out too interesting. You have to find another way to say it.

Well, now I'm gonna go and do my oaths homework! Ha ha ha!

THURSDAY SEPTEMBER 10TH

Caroline Hunter has a baby picture of herself up on Facebook that looks like she slept in curlers and is entering a baby beauty

pageant. Half the girls in our class have baby pictures of themselves up on Facebook, but it is against mine and Anna's rules. We think it's too cute-sy. It doesn't matter how much of a joke you try to make out of it, at some level you're saying, *'Look how adorable I was – love me!'* Our rule for our blog is no baby photos or sexy poses – both those are try-hard – only photos of us doing silly stuff.

Oh, I'd better explain about our blog. We are going to have the usual things like Favourite Colour (Me: Blue; Anna: Orange) and Favourite Book (Me: *His Dark Materials*; Anna: *Crime and Punishment). Crime and Punishment* is a big book with small writing and foreign names. I gave up reading it after three pages but Anna has very grown-up taste in books because of coming from a family of intellectuals. She is not intellectual herself – her marks are worse than mine – but she is under the influence of intellectuals like I am under the influence of telly. At Anna's house there is no telly!

When I found that out I said, 'But your Dad's *on* telly!'

Her whole family laughed though I was not trying to be funny. I just thought someone *on* telly must *have* a telly. Her Dad is an economist – he doesn't have a show on telly, but sometimes he makes documentaries and sometimes he is on the news, talking about economical things and waving his hand at those money charts which go up and down like hills and valleys. Especially recently he's on the telly because *everyone* is talking about

the recession and they need experts like him to say why it happened and how we can end it.

Sometimes my mum calls me, saying, 'Anna's dad is on the telly'.

I think she hopes I will learn something, but, sorry, it's impossible to know what he's on about.

Anyway, back to our blog; we want to put our marvellous adventures up on it to set us apart from all the other teenage bloggers. But we haven't had any marvellous adventures yet. So we were round at Anna's today trying to think of ideas. The Lotto numbers today were her mum and Charlie and Renata. Renata is at college now but obviously nobody at college has to work too hard because it seems like she spends all day sitting round the kitchen and all night going out. We cleared a space at the kitchen table to make our list. The kitchen table is also quite like the Lotto numbers because you never know what's going to be on it. There could be books or make-up from Renata, or sports clothes from Tommy (*sweaty* sports clothes!! Ugh!), or Anna's homework (she does have a desk in her room but she doesn't like working in her room, she says it's lonely) and there are always a few of Charlie's toys and his abandoned plastic plates of squashed banana. The whole house is like that: chaos. My mother wouldn't allow it, but then there are only four people in our house and none of them are sweaty boys. But I feel relaxed in Anna's house because if I broke something or spilled

juice, nobody would even notice.

Anyway, Anna wrote down two ideas for our blog:

1) Start a business.

(I said, what business? She said that's what we had to work out.)

2) Do something to raise money for charity.

(Anna has a good social conscience. It is part of coming under the influence of intellectuals, I think).

I wasn't sure about these ideas. I said they sounded like work, and what our parents do, not like a blog.

Anna said, 'Well what are *your* ideas then?' (quite rudely).

I said I had two ideas too:

1) We could go bungee jumping.

2) We could swim with dolphins.

That's when Renata did her Snort, Swivel, Swat routine:

'Who wants to read about you two flapping round, trying *pathetically* to commune with nature? I thought you wanted *original* ideas. Do you know how many accounts there are of swimming with dolphins on the net? About a million. Do you know how many interesting accounts there are of swimming with dolphins on the net? Nil. Nada. And as for bungee jumping … unless the rope snaps, we're just not interested.'

We just gazed at her, and waited—

'Oh, Renata!' said her mum.

Anna said, 'You think of something then!' and pushed her lip

out the way she does when she's angry.

Renata said, 'Well, let's see. Bullying? Vandalising? Shoplifting? That's all people want to read from teenagers.'

Her mum: '*Renata!*' – not in an *Oh, Renata!* voice this time, in a really cross voice. Renata went back down to her book.

Her mum said, 'Would you two take Charlie out to the garden? He needs fresh air.'

Charlie is the cutest baby in the world. He is very smart. He says 'Actually' a lot, which makes him sound grown-up though he is only two: 'Actually, I don't like apples.'

FRiDAY SEPTEMBER 11TH

I don't think the boys are fancying Heeun. You can normally tell when they fancy the new girl because they just keep going up to her. One of them will come up and tell her something and then another will come up to show her something and then another will come up to invite her to something. It's like the action of a magnet that we studied in science. But Heeun is like the negative bit of the magnet. No boys are coming up to her. She is repelling them. I am surprised because she is definitely pretty. But then I've noticed before that who the girls think is pretty is not always who the boys think is pretty. The boys' taste always infects the girls though. The first day of school Caroline Hunter was saying how pretty Heeun was and smarmy-ing up to her; now she's backing off because it's looking like Heeun is not going to be one

of the popular ones. It's impossible to be very popular if the boys don't fancy you.

In case you are wondering if me and Anna are popular, then yes we are, but not like that – I mean not envy-able popular. The boys don't automatically fancy us, and the girls don't want to be us, but they all like us (I think!). Actually, Anna has a boyfriend. It's just that she never sees him. Well it's Carl, who's in our class, so she *sees* him (every day in fact) but she never spends any time with him. They have been going out since the end of last term. But you wouldn't know it. In the summer we hung out with him and his friends a bit. But since we're back at school, nothing – they hardly even *talk*. But if you asked her, she'd say yeah, she's going out with Carl, but she'd say it in a completely uninterested voice. She is definitely not crazy about him. She isn't even *pathological* about him. She isn't even *neurotic* about him. She isn't even *hung up* on him.

It's not surprising. He is a total dud. His school trousers are slightly too short for his legs so you can see his ankles when he walks. It gives me a shivery, dreadful feeling every time I catch sight of those bony ankles. I can't see how Anna could have kissed him, but possibly neither can she seeing as how now she ignores him. But when there's a kissing opportunity, like at a party, she does use him for that still.

I think it's that she's a very practical person and she doesn't like wasting time or opportunities, so she will use him for kissing

till she replaces him.

This makes her sound ruthless, but she's not like an Exploiter. I mean he seems quite happy with the situation.

I am not that practical – there are not too many boys I want to kiss, and the ones I *do* want to kiss I am nervous about approaching, and if I *did* actually kiss them, I would probably become hung up-neurotic-pathological-crazy about them all at once and would never be able to set up such a slick/ruthless/convenient arrangement as Anna's.

I have kissed boys – well, I kissed one, in Irish College. Which counts, I guess, but it only *just* counts because it is part of the rules of Irish College that you learn to kiss. It's Rule 4 and it comes after Rule 3, Learn how to use the Genitive Case … So because it's part of the rules, well, you just grab the nearest male. I can hardly remember the name of the guy I kissed. Well, okay, he was called Mark. But I can't remember anything else about him. Well, okay, his tongue went frantic looking for something in my mouth. So, okay, I can remember the kiss, but not *him* specifically …

We haven't come up with anything for our blog yet. Maybe Renata is right – I am imagining a different me and Anna who bully and shoplift and vandalise. We could call ourselves Bomb and Demise and wear black all the time. I wonder if David Leydon has ever shoplifted? I think when he is not in his uniform he probably wears black.

Steak for dinner. Quite healthy. Justine was not eating much of hers so I ate it. Justine is a year younger than me, she is twelve.

The reason I have hardly mentioned her before is that she is deeply boring. She is as boring as my parents. Sorry. That sounds very mean. But Anna's mum said we had to admit *everything* to our diary, all our *innermost* thoughts, even the *bad* ones. When we were little me and Justine played together a lot but that was because: a) I didn't know how boring my house was then, and b) when she was little she was cute. It is only recently she has become deeply boring. She is quiet as a mouse in the house. You wouldn't even know she's around most of the time.

MONDAY SEPTEMBER 14TH

Anna has had an idea for our blog. It is an idea based on her original idea – to start a business. Our business is going to be to organise children's birthday parties. People will hire us to arrange party games and keep hordes of children amused for three hours. Anna had this idea because her neighbour asked her to help out with her six year old's birthday. So Anna did pass the parcel and pin the tail on the donkey and musical bumps and organised the singing of Happy Birthday. She was very good at it, she says, and stopped the Girl Who Lost Musical Bumps from crying, and then cheated a bit to make sure the Birthday Boy won pass the parcel. Afterwards the neighbour gave her €25 and big thanks and this gave Anna the idea to

make it a business, not just a one-off.

I do not like to pour scorn on my best friend's ideas, but I was Not Impressed. It didn't sound like much of an idea for a blog.

I said (in my best impersonation of Renata), 'Who wants to read about us playing pass the parcel with a load of six year olds?'

Anna said, 'Maybe something will go wrong and it will be a comedy blog.'

I said, 'We can't go into it hoping something will go wrong!'

She said, 'We won't be *hoping* something will go wrong! It just *will*, that's what happens with kids. The Birthday Boy will vomit, or some little pig will smear chocolate cake all over the Little Princess's pink party dress.'

So then I started to laugh, although I didn't want to because once you start to laugh, you've lost the argument, but it was the thought of a Fat Little Princess in Pigtails with dark chocolate smears all down her frilly pink dress, bawling … ha!

But then I recovered with a good argument, 'Yeah, well, we can't put that on the blog though! People will find out and not hire us!'

Anna said, 'Oh shut up! We'll make money anyway!'

This, as they say in Anna's house, was UN-ANSWER-ABLE.

Apparently we are going to charge €60 for our services. This seems a lot to me, but Anna says it's not because we will have to arrange all the party games beforehand, and wrap the Parcel, and fill the Going Home Bags and choose the music (big deal!) If we

do the food, it's extra apparently, €20 extra, because cutting sandwiches and making rice crispy cakes can take forever (true!)

I said, 'Who is going to spend €80 on a six-year-old's party???'

Anna said, 'You'd be surprised!'

Apparently it costs way more to rent one of those leisure centres for parties – you pay more than €15 per child! Well, OK, I *am* surprised …

Anna is making up posters to advertise our services.

WEDNESDAY SEPTEMBER 16TH

A mad thing happened at lunchtime today. Emma came up to us and said, 'Will you do something to Elaine for me? She was mean to me.'

Elaine is in our class. She is fine, I guess, but deeply boring, except that she has a bad temper. When she loses her temper, it is *not* deeply boring! I guess she lost it with Emma, and Emma is like jelly, she's so nervous, but still – we were amazed. What did she want *us* to do about it?

But Anna said, 'We'll think about it,' in a grand voice.

When Emma went off we were laughing because we couldn't believe it.

I said, 'She's crazy, but maybe we're like Robin Hood, protecting the weak. Emma is definitely the Weak and Elaine is the Strong.'

Anna said, 'If we do do something mean, she'll have to pay us,

we'll be risking our necks for her.'

I said, 'Yeah', though Robin Hood didn't get paid, I don't think, but then he only worked for the Poor, and Emma is not the Poor. She gets quite a lot of pocket money.

Anna hardly gets any pocket money, which is why she is always thinking of ways to earn it. I don't know why she hardly gets any pocket money when she lives in a big house. Maybe because a) she has too many brothers and sisters so there isn't any money left over, or b) her parents are against pocket money like they are against telly, or c) the recession stopped her pocket money. The recession hasn't stopped my pocket money yet but it has entered our house – the words 'we can't afford it' are now used quite a lot. For instance I want an iPod but 'we can't afford it' and we only went for one week to France this year because we 'couldn't afford' the second week and Dad 'couldn't afford' more time off work. If the recession is forcing an entry into my house, it has probably taken over Anna's, since that's her Dad's job. I'm pretty sure she's so obsessed about starting a business because she's afraid that all the money is leaking out of the country and can only be halted by people starting up new businesses (well I think this is what her Dad says).

We still haven't thought of anything to do to Elaine yet.

THURSDAY SEPTEMBER 17TH

We are going to hide Elaine's gym bag. I thought of this. It's

quite clever – she will get into trouble, but not *too* much trouble, and no one will know it's us. We told Emma what we were going to do and Anna said, 'That will cost you €9.50,' in a very professional voice.

(Apparently €9.50 is the psychologically correct way to ask for €10). Emma said OK!

FRIDAY SEPTEMBER 18TH

At break we found Elaine's gym bag by the lockers and took it away and hid it beside the upstairs toilets in the store-room where the cleaning ladies keep the cleaning things.

At gym later on Elaine couldn't find her gym bag. First she was confused, and then she began to lose her temper. She stomped about, throwing things around, trying to uncover her bag. The rest of us all changed into our sports gear and then Mrs Moloney (our gym teacher) arrived and said to Elaine what was the problem? Was she sick?

Elaine shouted then, really loudly, 'NO! I'm not sick! My bag is gone! Someone must have stolen it!!'

She is extremely fierce when she loses her temper.

Mrs Moloney didn't give out to her. She said, 'All right, Elaine, well, have a good look for it. Maybe you left it at home?'

'I did NOT leave it at home!!' shouted Elaine.

Then Mrs Moloney said sharply, 'Calm down. Take another

look and then you'd better go to Study.'

So we left Elaine and went and picked teams for netball. Anna was one of the first to be picked. She is good at sport. Well, she is not particularly fast at running, but she is very good at throwing and catching and kicking – hand-eye coordination, it's called. She throws the ball like a boy, over-arm. I bowl it under-arm. I am not so gifted with hand-eye coordination, but I am good at gymnastics because I'm pretty bendy, I can do cartwheels and handstands and I'm brave – I have no fear of vaulting over the horse (on which Emma, for instance, always gets stuck!) But that's not much use in netball. Luckily Anna got me picked so I wasn't left till last. It is highly embarrassing to be left till last.

I played safe making little passes for other people to sort out, but I missed quite a few balls, I admit. I thought about Elaine stomping her way to study and I was glad she lost her temper because it made me not have to be (too) sorry for her or feel (too) guilty.

Afterwards I asked Anna, shouldn't Elaine know that it was because of what she did to Emma that her gym bag disappeared, otherwise how would she learn her lesson? But Anna said no, it was Karma and she'd start to understand that herself. I asked what 'Karma' was, and Anna said it was the circle of your deeds: if you do something good, it comes back round to you, and if you do something bad, it came back round to you as well. It's Indian philosophy apparently. I said, well maybe we'd better tell Elaine

about Karma so she knows what's going on. Then Anna got annoyed and said that wasn't necessary, Karma happened *anyway* whether you knew what it was or not, and you understood it subconsciously.

Subconsciously! That proved it – she didn't know what she was talking about, it was something she got from home. In Anna's house they are always talking about subconscious-es, and unconscious-es and conscience-s. This is sigh-chiatrists' language.

I said, 'If Karma happens *anyway*, then how come it wouldn't have happened to Elaine if we hadn't *made* it happen?'

I said it in an arguing way, but Anna started to laugh and said, 'Sometimes you have to give Karma a big, fat shove!'

'Yeah,' I said, 'and sometimes you have to hide the Gym Bag of Karma!'

So then Anna howled and shoved me, 'Stupid!'

We were doubled up in hysterics, but Anna managed to say grandly between the hysterics, 'We are the Instruments of Karma!', which made us have *more* hysterics.

SUNDAY SEPTEMBER 20TH

So now we have two businesses! As 'The Party People' we arrange children's parties. As 'The Instruments of Karma' we do nasty things to people who deserve it.

We have made up a poster for The Party People. It goes like this:

THE PARTY PEOPLE!

Is it your kid's birthday? Dreading the day? Have you time to: cut sandwiches, ice cakes, chocolate-cover rice crispies, wrap the parcel, draw the donkey, fill the Goody Bags...? Can you cope with crying kids, hair pulling, snotty noses, ripped dresses, food fights ...?

Or is the thought bringing you out in a COLD SWEAT?

Have no fear! **THE PARTY PEOPLE** will take it out of your hands! We will: cut sandwiches, ice cakes, wrap the parcel, draw the donkey, fill Goody Bags. And we'll also: dry tears, wipe noses, brush hair, mend dresses, and lead the singing of Happy Birthday...
(Oh and we'll clear up too!)

Prices on request – lower than the Leisureplexes!

Call Anna and Denise, two very responsible 2nd Years with huge experience
(references available on request)

That's just the text – we are going to add pictures, of course. It is quite a good text, I think. We worked it all out in Anna's kitchen yesterday. Renata helped. She got quite into it. We kind of suspected she might which is why we started on it in the

kitchen. Renata is actually a genius. She was queen of the school until she left last year. Just the way she wore her uniform you could tell she had a very wild, funky and original fashion sense. And everything she wrote in the school magazine was wild, funky and original as well. Me and Anna know that she is actually a BITCH, but Anna also thinks she is brilliant, which makes her a brilliant bitch, I guess. But anyway we did want her help for our poster.

In the beginning we were just listing the games we'd organise and making it sound like fun, but then Renata cut in, 'No! Cut the fun – you need the Climate of Fear!'

We said, 'Climate of Fear?'

'Ummm, yeah, make 'em scared, that's how to sell it – snotty noses, black eyes, tears before bedtime, mess, mess and more mess. Terrify the house-proud!'

Apparently if people feel nervous, they're more likely to buy their way out of the problem. But they want to get a deal too, so, 'Undercut the leisureplexes,' said Renata.

Anna's mum said, 'Oh, Renata! That's all so cynical!'

Renata said, 'That's life.'

This afternoon we showed the poster to my mum. Anna phoned to say she was coming round to my house, so I said automatically, 'No, I'll come round to yours.'

She said, 'No, we *always* go to mine, let's go to yours, I'm fed up of mine.'

I was surprised. My house is deeply boring and hers is the Lotto numbers – why would she rather go to mine? But since it's true, we do always go to hers, I had to give in. My parents were out shopping when she arrived. There was just Justine watching telly in our front room, which was clean and tidy as usual. Our house is okay. There is nothing very unique about it. Possibly you could use it in an ad for, say, breakfast cereal or washing-up powder or yoghurt. There's nothing to alarm you in any of the corners – no dirty runners, or discarded coats, or broken toys, or just mess like there is in Anna's house. But you couldn't use it in an ad for mobile phones or bottled beer or anything cool because, for instance, we don't have a long sunny room with a long white sofa where girls with shiny nails can cuddle boys with stubble. Anna chatted to Justine till I dragged her upstairs to my room.

Then she sat on the twirly chair by my desk and twirled round in circles criticising the posters on my walls: '*That* has to go' (twirl), and 'that's so *last* year' (twirl), and 'not *more* dolphins!' (twirl), until I said, 'You sound like Renata' and she said, 'No!' and I said, 'Yes! It must be contagious or maybe it's in your genes,' and she said, 'No!'

But I could see that secretly she was *flattered* to sound like Renata.

Then she said, 'Why don't we ask Justine what she thinks of The Party People?'

I said, 'What would she know?' and Anna said, 'Now, *you*

29

sound like Renata.'

Then we heard my mum come in and Anna insisted we go down and show her the poster. Mum was really impressed actually, she laughed and laughed at the poster. Then she said she'd make us up business cards at work. They will be condensed versions of the poster.

Mum said, 'A card travels faster than a poster, it travels from hand to hand.'

She is right, and we are very pleased, actually.

We are not doing up a poster or business cards for the Instruments of Karma – of course not! It is top secret. But Anna thought if Emma was ready to pay us to be mean to someone, other people would too. We are going to spread our services by word of mouth. I think Anna is mostly interested by the extra cash. I am mostly interested because suddenly I realised: this could work for the blog! As the Instruments of Karma, we will have marvellous adventures that people will want to read about. Of course we can't put our real names – we'll be Demise and Bomb, under cover of secrecy. But that could make it *more* fun. We are going to put up cunning photos of the backs – or sides – of our heads, so you can't really make out who we are. I think this blog may have a cult following.

MONDAY SEPTEMBER 21ST

Emma paid us today. €9.50. She said, 'It was *great* when Mrs

Moloney got mad with Elaine!'

I thought she was a bit too enthusiastic about this! But then she *is* Elaine's victim.

She said, 'Shouldn't Elaine know that it was because of being mean to me she got into trouble?'

So I said, in a 'talking-to-an-idiot' voice, 'No. It's Karma.'

As the Instruments of Karma, we also lend money. But with Interest. Interest means you get back more money than you loaned.

This happened because at lunch Pierce asked did I have a lend of €5 and I was about to say 'yes', when Anna said, 'Yes, but that will be 10 per cent interest', so Pierce and I both said, 'Interest?' and she said, 'That means you have to pay back €5.50.'

Pierce thought this was quite funny. He said, 'Sure'.

Lending is a *subsidiary* of our main business, Anna says. We are *branching* out. I think that these are economical terms she gets from her father. Our main business – being nasty to people who deserve it – is the trunk of the tree, but branches can grow from the trunk. I think a tree is a good image for the Instruments of Karma. I think we should draw one, and then photocopy it on loads of pages and whenever we do something nasty we can leave a photocopy of the Karmic Tree at the scene of the crime.

We can get Tommy to draw the tree. Tommy is very good at art *and* music *and* acting. He is not an intellectual genius like Renata and John (John is Anna's eldest brother. I don't really

know him, but he's obviously very smart because a) he's at Oxford now, and b) all the teachers are always asking Anna about him in an interested way). Tommy is just average in school, like Anna. But he played Puck in *A Midsummer's Night Dream* last year and he was AMAZING. And he's in a band. And he's pretty good-looking, so all the girls in the school are in love with him. I might be in love with him too, but he's Anna's brother so if I was in love with him then every time I saw him I'd blush and stammer which would make going round to her house not easy.

But Anna is not sure about the Karmic Tree. She says it might compromise our anonymity. I don't see how it can if we don't put our names. I think it's good to have a symbol. Like a panda (that means World Wild Life Fund) or a Shamrock (that means Ireland), or a tick 'yes' (that means Nike). I like these symbols. The tree can be the homepage of our blog, so people say *what's this?* Then they click on a branch and a photo of me and Anna in black silhouette will come up and a description of whatever nasty thing we did.

We need to get going on this blog. But Anna is not so into it as me. She is only thinking about new branches for our business that will make us more money.

WEDNESDAY SEPTEMBER 23RD

Just back from Anna's. It is late. They asked me to stay over for

dinner! We were sitting in the kitchen and there were these delicious smells from the oven and maybe her mum saw me looking longingly over because she said, 'Would you like to stay for dinner?'

So then I was extremely helpful about peeling potatoes and everything.

Guess what was for dinner? It was *ostrich* stew! I am not joking, but I thought *they* were joking when they said it. It was a very nice stew but it tasted like any stew, I mean like beef or lamb stew, but then Anna's mum and dad started a very long conversation all about the ostrich and did it work in the stew.

Anna's dad said, 'Not as good as the antelope,' and Anna's mum said, 'The antelope was *dry*,' then Anna joined in and said, 'The venison was best.'

I was trying to keep up. I said, 'What is venison?' and they all said, 'Deer.'

It sounded like a zoo. Ostriches and antelopes and deer. I mean, I know there are deer in Phoenix Park, but I didn't think you're allowed to eat them and I was sure there were no antelopes, and *definitely* no ostriches anywhere in Ireland.

So I said, 'Did you get it from the zoo?'

So then they all laughed. (I meant them to.)

Anna's mum said, no, the antelope was imported, but the ostrich came from an ostrich farm outside Dublin. I said *no way!* I really want to see this farm!

Then I said, 'But what's wrong with beef?'

Anna said, 'Renata doesn't eat beef.'

Renata said, 'No, I don't eat intensively-farmed animals that have been reared on the meat of other intensively-farmed animals with the result that their herbivorous systems implode through cannibalism.'

She sounded very passionate. Tommy was across the table from me, and he gave me his smile – the girls at school go *crazy* over his smile – and said, 'She's afraid of Mad Cow Disease.'

He knew I didn't know what she was on about.

It is pretty typical that the *whole* of Anna's family has to change what they eat just because Renata is scared of getting some disease that nobody ever gets except for a very few people in the English newspapers years ago.

But then Anna's dad said, 'It's good to diversify. Good for your system to vary its diet' – He looked straight at me. He has very piercing eyes so it seemed like his eyes were piercing my belly and he could see right into my system that doesn't actually have a varied diet, but just chicken, and hamburgers and fishfingers – 'and it's good for farming to diversify too. Interesting experiment, this ostrich farm. If it works we'll have another market.'

Tommy said, 'I don't think it's gonna catch on. Maybe if something happened to cows ...'

'Disgusting things,' said Renata violently, 'they should all be

slaughtered. Destroying the ozone layer with their *farts*.'

'It's not *their* fault,' said Anna.

Anna likes animals. And she was right. Renata is a very unreasonable person. How can you blame cows for *farting*? And anyway, how can farts destroy the ozone layer? *Aeroplanes* destroy the ozone layer. I think maybe Renata is going nuts.

Afterwards I did loads of clearing up to make sure they'd ask me to stay for dinner again. I started clearing the table without being asked. Anna had to be *forced* into her job. Then Renata dropped me home because she wants to practise her driving. But her mum had to come in the car with us because she's not allowed to go out without an experienced driver yet. I don't think she ever should be. I am lucky to be at home in my bed alive.

THURSDAY SEPTEMBER 24TH

We have got our first job as The Party People! Someone who works with mum wants us to do her daughter's party next week. Her daughter is going to be six. She wants us to do everything – food and games – so that's €80! We have to call round this Saturday to their house and get money to buy food and things for the Going Home Bags. Anna has brought a book with lined pages and written ACCOUNTS on the first page. She says we have to account for every penny we spend.

We have not got another job as Instruments of Karma yet, but

then we aren't able to advertise it the way we advertise The Party People. So how are people to hear about us? I am a bit worried about this.

FRIDAY SEPTEMBER 25TH

Trouble. Pierce is not paying us back our interest! He came up to me at break and said, 'Here's the €5' so Anna said, quick as you like, 'And the 50 cent?'

He said, 'You were joking about that, right?' and she said, 'Do I look like I'm laughing?'

She didn't. Her jaw was out and her eyes were narrow.

He said in a rough, unpleasant, jeering voice, 'Who d'you think you are? The Bank of Ireland?'

'You agreed. We had a deal.'

He said, 'Deal? Sch-meal', which wasn't a very quick-witted thing to say, but then he isn't very quick-witted.

Then he said, 'Anyway I didn't borrow it from *you*, I borrowed it from Denise, and she's cool with it, right?' and he turned to me, smiling, so I said, very fast, 'No, I'm with Anna.'

'Yeah, I should have known, you're just a sheep.' He turned and walked away.

I shouted after him, 'She's my *accountant*.'

And Anna shouted, 'You're a toxic loan! You're why this country is going down the tubes!'

Then we both stood there in a RAGE. Anna said, 'He *agreed*.

He thinks he's above the law, leaving it to us to bail him out.'

I ignored her; she was just quoting her dad.

I said, 'I'm not a *sheep*!'

She said, 'Next time we'll have to draw up a contract.'

I said, 'Who do you think you are? The Bank of Ireland?' because now *I* was pissed off with her.

In fact I agreed with Pierce. It's stupid to charge interest. But if I agreed with Pierce, why did I say I was with Anna? Maybe because I am a sheep after all? This is a really depressing thought.

Finally she saw I was mad. She said impatiently, 'Oh, come *on*, why d'you care what he says? You know what you are. You don't have to base your opinion of yourself on what other people think.'

Then I felt better. It's true that maybe from the outside it *looks* like I'm a sheep because of Anna having such a strong character, but from inside, where we are, that's not what I am. We are actually quite equal.

Anna went on, 'Maybe you don't agree about charging him interest. But he agreed to it. He *knew* what he was getting into. And now he's broken his word. He just went along with it to get what he wanted.'

I said sarcastically, 'Yeah, well, big surprise, he's a liar as well as a bully.' Then I added grandly, 'We shouldn't do business with such people,' so Anna had to laugh.

She said, 'Zero credit rating!' whatever that means.

Then she said, 'We shouldn't let him away with it.'

I said, 'No-o-o', but I didn't sound very sure because how do you stop someone like Pierce doing what he wants?

SATURDAY SEPTEMBER 26TH

This has been a *very* long day. I almost don't have energy to write.

After lunch Anna came round 'cause Mum had offered to drive us to Mrs Mahony's. That is the woman she works with whose daughter is having her birthday. When we got there, I said to Mum, 'We have to go in just by ourselves because it's our job.'

I thought it would make us look like little kids if Mum was with us. So she said fine, she'd wait in the car at the end of the road.

Mrs Mahony's house was in an estate. It was big and new. All the houses were identical and very clean. They all had very clean front gardens with perfect lawns and big driveways with new cars. Our car is quite clean, but it's also quite old. But then I remembered that Anna's garden is not neat at all, it has messy flowers and Charlie's toys on the lawn. So then I felt better. It was weird, though, that everyone's house here was perfect.

You'd think there would be *one* messy family.

I said to Anna, 'Do you think you have to pass a Clean Test to live here?'

So then she looked round, and got what I meant immediately,

and she said, 'No, there's a Clean Committee, and you get three chances, and the first two times you get a warning, but the next time you don't wash your car, you're *out*,' and she waved her hand in a dramatic *out* gesture.

We were both giggling when we walked into No.17 – Mrs Mahony's – but then I looked at her gleaming windows, and I said, 'God, how are we gonna make it clean enough after the party?' and Anna suddenly looked alarmed because actually she is really lazy about clearing up.

We didn't look at each other when we rang the bell. My heart was beating fast. But Mrs Mahony seemed quite nice.

She said, 'Oh, Anna and Denise, The Party People,' and brought us through to the kitchen.

She was quite young, and she had very neat hair, like it was just blow-dried, which is what I expected from her house. Inside was just as clean as outside. It was just perfect.

We chatted about the party and what games we should do. Anna said Pass the Parcel and Pin the Tail on the Donkey and Musical Bumps and Musical Statues and Mrs Mahony kept nodding. I said, what about outside games, because I was looking out the window and they had a big back garden and I remembered that children need Fresh Air. I think something terrible happens to them if they don't get Fresh Air.

Mrs Mahony said, 'Ye-e-ss', like that, a very long *Ye-e-ess* 'but,' she said, 'not *rough* games!' so I knew she was worrying

about her lawn.

Then she said, 'Now how much do you need for food and going home bags, and, oh, prizes?'

I saw Anna's face. It was looking panic-stricken, just like mine probably. How much did we need? We never discussed how much to charge for buying stuff.

Anna cleared her throat. She looked at me, then she said firmly, 'Forty euro.'

I nodded.

Mrs Mahony said, 'That should be fine,' and took out forty euro from her purse and gave it to Anna.

We were quite pleased with ourselves when we got back to the car. I asked Mum would she mind driving us to the shopping centre so we could buy stuff for the party.

Mum said, 'How much did she give you?'

I told her about the forty euro.

Mum said, '*Forty euro*. You have to buy all the food and the prizes and the going-home bags for forty euro?'

We said yes.

Mum said, 'And the cake?'

We looked at each other, and nodded.

'That *woman*,' said Mum. She was nearly laughing, but cross too. 'I'd better go in for you and get more money.'

I said, '*No!* That would be so embarrassing!'

And Anna said, 'It's the recession! Everyone has to budget!'

So Mum sighed and said, 'Lambs to the slaughter!' almost to herself, and then, 'Well, I guess they have to make their own mistakes.' And she drove off, thank God! It would have been mortifying if she'd gone in!

At the shopping centre, I said, 'Thank you very much, we'll get the bus home.'

She said, 'I'd better come in and supervise the shopping. You'll need to budget.'

But me and Anna said *'No!'* so she kind of laughed and shrugged, but as we were leaving, she called out, 'You'll have to make the cake. You won't be able to afford one.'

Anna said, 'Put your phone on calculator. We've got to add everything up,' so I knew she was worried Mum was right and we wouldn't have enough money.

Well, the shopping was ... well, like a rollercoaster. First it was fine. We got the crisps and they cost, like, nothing. Well actually, they cost €3.50. (I know exactly what *everything* costs). So that made us happy and loud and boastful.

'Huh,' said Anna, 'we've *loads* of money!'

'*Yeah,*' I said, 'we'll probably have some left *over!*'

That was the rollercoaster going up.

But then after we'd got the chocolate and the biscuits and the sweets and the popcorn and the Coke and the bread for sandwiches and the cheese and ham, we were way up. My phone calculator said €34.

'Well,' said Anna, 'that's okay. I guess we'll make the cake like your mum said ...'

'Going away presents and prizes!' I cried tragically. I stopped in the aisle and put my hand on my brow in a tragic actress way, because it was pretty funny really.

But Anna was losing her sense of humour, 'Oh for God's sake!' she shouted.

That was the rollercoaster plunging down.

She was looking for someone to blame, but there was no blaming me.

I could see the black cloud coming over her though, so I said, 'Value brands?'

And she said, 'I guess ...'

So then we had to run around swapping the famous brands for the supermarket value brands. There wasn't a value brand for everything, but (for your information!) there are incredible savings on ham and cheese. And then we got Ribena concentrate instead of Coke (they were only six, they wouldn't notice, and anyway Coke is bad for them) and we got the corn kernels instead of the ready-made popcorn. So then my calculator said †27.

'That is a significant saving,' said Anna gravely. (Rollercoaster up!) We decided we'd make the cake using flour and butter and stuff from my house or Anna's. So that left €13 for prizes and going-home bags, which seemed quite a lot.

'Let's go to the joke shop,' I said.

On the way out from the shopping centre, I saw the new boy, David Leydon! He was hanging out with three other guys not from our school. And he *was* wearing black! I was right about that.

I nudged Anna. 'Look, there's David Leydon.'

She looked across, 'Oh yeah …'

Then she just started walking towards him, me after her. If I'd been on my own I wouldn't have dared, but Anna is a) very brave, and b) never gets pathological-neurotic over boys so she never gets nervous. (Does this mean – because I got nervous – that I fancy David Leydon??)

We walked up and stood there and said, 'Hi.'

He looked at us and said, 'Oh, hi…' not very enthusiastically, but not unfriendly – not anything really.

It seemed like he was much older than us, which he can't be. He is taller, maybe that's it.

We stood there, but he didn't introduce us to his friends, so I said, 'What are you up to?'

He said, 'You know, hanging out …'

There was silence. I thought his friends were sniggering, but I wasn't looking directly at them. Then he seemed to realise it was *his* turn to ask the question.

So he said, 'What about you?'

I said, 'We're going to the joke shop.'

'Yeah?'

'Yeah…'

One of his friends said, 'Early Hallowe'en?'

Then Anna said, 'No, we're organising a children's party.'

I was embarrassed then. I went a bit red. It suddenly seemed a kiddie thing to do.

But the friend said, 'Oh right. Getting paid?'

So I said quickly, 'Yes, we have a *business* running parties.'

It is certainly not kiddie to be earning money, and I thought they looked a bit impressed.

Then Anna said, 'Yeah, and we have to get on with it.'

So I said, 'See you' and we walked off.

Anna said, 'Well, they were interesting!' sarcastically.

She is very hard on people, Anna. She really is. She is especially hard on boys.

I didn't want her to know that maybe – who knows? – I fancied David Leydon, so I said, 'Uh-huh'.

The joke shop was pricey. (Rollercoaster down!) Fake blood was €7! Also it seemed to have turned less into a joke shop and more into a sex shop. I mean, there was a little glass with 'I ♥ Sluts' on it and there was a bra made out of sweeties. These are not appropriate prizes for six-year-olds. But there was a plastic roll-y eyeball which you could pop in someone's tea so when they got to the end it would be staring up at them. It only cost €2 and it was a suitable prize for a six-year-old. We were just paying when

David Leydon and his friends came in! No joke! (Ha, ha!)

'How d'you get on?' said the one who asked about Hallowe'en.

He was leader, that was obvious, he was very confident.

'Not so good,' I said, but he was looking at Anna, so then I knew it was Anna who'd brought him to the shop. It is not very hard to work these things out. Boys like Anna. She is a bit of a tomboy and has quite short hair, but she's cute-looking.

That's what my mum said once, 'Anna is the cute type.'

'But she's not *cute*,' I told her, because babies are cute – Anna is tough!

My mum laughed, 'So don't judge people by their looks …'

I am not exactly the cute type. I don't know what type I am. Well, I am the skinny type. Some girls in the class have breasts and waists and thighs, but I just go straight up, straight down. Renata says I've got the opposite to an hour-glass figure – a pencil figure – because my chest, waist and thighs are all exactly the same circumference (this is a typical Renata exaggeration – actually my tummy sticks out *more* than my chest, ha!). My hair falls straight down too. It is light brown. I was a cute kid and people smiled at me for no reason in shops, but now my face is longer and has some spots and people smile less. But my eyes are quite large and an interesting colour – like green plums – and apparently loads of girls go through the gawky stage, that's my mum's word for it. It means the stage between being a cute kid

and a stunning sixth year (there are a lot of girls in our school at that stage, ha!)

When we all spilled back out onto the street, Hallowe'en Boy took charge.

'Let's see what you got.'

Then he asked us how much we had left to spend and when we told him, he laughed. All the others laughed too.

'Real big spender,' said Hallowe'en Boy. Then he said decisively, 'I know – the pound shop!'

'Two Euro shop now,' said David Leydon.

'Whatever,' said Anna, 'that's a good idea.'

So we all trooped off together. (Rollercoaster right up!) Hallowe'en Boy was talking in his confident way to Anna all about the Party Business, which was the obvious thing to talk about. I was beside David Leydon. He wasn't saying anything. I don't think he is very communicative. He is moody and surly just like a rock star.

I said, 'So what do you think of our school then?'

He said, 'It sucks, like all schools.'

'Oh. How many schools have you been to?'

'This is my third – including primary school.'

'Were you expelled?' I asked.

He said, 'No. Of course not. If I was expelled, other schools wouldn't accept me. I just didn't like them.'

He made me feel naïve, but I said, 'Why didn't you like them?'

Our conversation was actually going quite well, although it consisted of me asking all the questions. If I didn't ask questions, we'd dry up, that was sure.

At the pound (sorry €2!) shop, there were balloons and bubbles and keyrings and a whole load of cheap stuff, so we got prizes and things for the Going Home Bags. And we had 62 cent over! We had a laugh too. The pound (sorry €2!) shop is full of stupid gadgets to laugh at.

Outside the shop, Hallowe'en Boy said, 'OK, girls, business over. Now let's go to McDonald's.'

But one of the others said, 'Not McDonald's' and Anna said, 'We don't have any money left!' I looked at Hallowe'en Boy and said 'Unless you know a 62 cent café?'

Everyone laughed. (I meant them to). Then we hung about the corner a bit but in the end we just went off. They were gonna hang round town some more. I'd have stayed with them, but Anna decided to go, and I wasn't gonna stay alone – obviously!

I said, 'So they weren't *that* bad,' because I wanted to talk about them.

Anna said, 'Keith is enterprising. The rest are goons.'

Keith is Hallowe'en Boy. It's a pity she doesn't like David Leydon, but actually it's not *that* much of a pity.

MONDAY SEPTEMBER 28TH

Uh-oh. Just had a fight. Have been sent up to my room. Like a

five-year-old! Am SEETHING!

What happened was I was called down for dinner and when I got there it was pizza.

I said, 'Oh-hh *pizza!* and my mum said, 'Something wrong with pizza?' It was her warning voice, and really I suppose I should have been warned, but I wasn't because a) it is important to speak your mind and not be down-trodden in Life and b) pizza is not so healthy, and it is important for the *whole* family that we eat more healthily. I wasn't just thinking of me. I was thinking of Dad and Justine as well!

So I said, 'Pizza doesn't have a lot of nutritional value. Not like ostrich.' But I sat down and was actually ready to eat because a) I like pizza and b) there was salad with it and salad is Healthy.

So if mum had just left it at that like she should have there wouldn't have been an argument, but she said, 'Ostrich?'

Her voice was gone from warning to dangerous, and I was scared. I have to admit. She can still scare me. I didn't say anything. Neither did anyone else. Justine was just staring at her plate.

Mum said, 'And where did you have ostrich?'

I said, in a very *casual* voice, not a scared voice, 'Oh, at Anna's.'

She said, 'I see. And it's now beneath you to eat pizza?'

I said, 'Well, it's important to diversify. I think our diet in this house is quite monotonous.'

I was proud of using 'monotonous' in the right way and I

spoke in a nice, explaining voice, not a bratty one, because maybe Mum didn't realise how monotonous our diet is. I was trying to help!

But Dad said, 'Apologise to your mother.' Just like that, in a heavy, no-argument voice.

I said, 'But I'm not saying anything *wrong*. I'm just saying that maybe–'

He cut me off then. 'Apologise immediately or go upstairs.' So what choice did I have? I stood up and slammed back my chair and went upstairs, banging the door. And then I burst into tears.

I am *so* mad. I was trying to help and they treat me like a little kid. Why shouldn't I be allowed an opinion on what we eat? Is this some kind of insane boarding school where the Headmistress' word is Law, and you get beaten just for asking questions? At Anna's house everyone gets to speak their mind freely. Probably if *Charlie* said he didn't like his dinner, he wouldn't have to eat it.

Am very hungry now. Not sure what to do. I need a hidden stash of food in my room. I will find myself apologising when I don't really mean it just because I'm starving. They are trying to break my spirit through hunger!

WEDNESDAY SEPTEMBER 30TH

Cows' farts *do* destroy the ozone layer! In Geography today we

were doing all about the environment and Mrs Finch asked what destroys the ozone layer so I put up my hand and said, 'Aeroplanes and cars', and she wrote it on the board.

Then someone else said, 'CFCs, you know, in fridges' and she wrote that down, then Anna said, 'Cows' farts!' so we all began to giggle, but Mrs Finch said 'Yes, unfortunately that is one of the biggest causes. They release methane gas,' So then she wrote down 'Methane gas from cows', which saved her having to write 'Cows' farts'.

I should have known Renata couldn't have got it wrong.

We discussed what to do to cut harmful gases, like using trains and bikes instead of cars, and boats instead of planes. We didn't work out what to do about the cows though. Nobody said, 'Slaughter them!', because nobody is a psychopath like Renata.

I said, 'Change their diet' because it is diet that causes farting, but everyone cracked up laughing.

Anna said, 'Yeah, put them in a concrete jungle!' so then I got why everyone was laughing.

Admittedly it could be hard to stop cows eating grass in Ireland!

This is a Conundrum.

At break Pierce went up to Charlie Nuttall and took his Mars bar. Just like that! Charlie had just pulled off the wrapper and was about to bite when Pierce appeared (ap*pierced*!) and leaned in and took the bar casually and said, 'Give us some of that!'

Charlie said, 'Uugh–' and then changed it to, 'uugh ... Uu ... no problem,' and watched while Pierce bit off an enormous bite – way more than half – and then handed it back to him, all covered with Pierce slobber.

'Ta,' said Pierce, and he gave Charlie's hair a ruffle, a really patronising ruffle, the way some grown-ups ruffle kids' hair, but I never would cause nobody likes being patronised, not even four-year-olds. And certainly not Charlie Nuttall. He looked frustrated and embarrassed that everyone had seen this but there was nothing he could do.

Anna said to me in a quiet voice, 'That's it. We're gonna have to get Pierce for lying to us and bullying too ... it's our duty.'

'A good dose of Karma for him,' I said enthusiastically, but I was nervous. Pierce is harder to get than Elaine. Maybe he's out-side the Karmic circle. I mean, if Karma was gonna get him for his bad deeds, surely it would have got him by now?

Oh, the pizza fight? Well, it was Resolved.

Dad came to my room and said, 'Do you not know that when someone makes food for you it is very rude to complain?'

I said, 'Of course. But *mum* made it.' I mean, of course I would never complain about a *stranger's* food.

He sighed and said, 'Denise, you are old enough to realise that your mother isn't a robot programmed to look after you. If she spends time cooking, it's the same as if a stranger does. You still have to be polite.'

I was going to argue because a) I am argumentative and b) how can Mum be the same as a stranger? (that's crazy talk – if you can't say exactly what you think at home, where can you?) and c) she didn't actually *make* the pizza, she just heated it up. But I didn't argue because a) I was *starving* and b) Dad looked like he was making an effort to control himself. He looked like one wrong word and he'd explode. He has been pretty bad-tempered recently because he's working too hard, because of the recession, I guess. He leaves earlier and he comes back later and he looks tired. So this time I read the warning signs.

I said, 'Okay, sorry' and then went down to Mum and said, 'Sorry,' and then I ate the pizza – and salad. So they did manage to break me through hunger! So now I know I would not be able to hold out long if I was being tortured in a death camp. I would give up all the information I knew after just one day's starvation. I ate Justine's remaining pizza too. She left about half of hers. How come she didn't get into trouble over that?

Just sent Anna a text:

boys darts – what to do?

She wrote back, really fast:

bull 'do

Which translates as: *cull 'em.* I am impressed how fast she thought of that. And it was good coincidence that '*bull*' came up for '*cull*'. Because of cows, you know.

FRIDAY OCTOBER 2ND

Went to Anna's house to make the cake. Her mum wasn't there. This turned out to be very unfortunate – for the cake, and for us. In fact we would have been better off going to my house like Anna wanted to because Mum makes good cakes, but I didn't want to so I said Mum wouldn't be there. This was not exactly a lie because she *might* have been shopping, but it wasn't exactly the truth either.

At Anna's, the only people we had to help us with the cake were Renata and her friend Alva. They were in a very silly mood, I could tell as soon as we went in. They started saying names of cakes back and forth to each other and the names got sillier and sillier:

Renata: 'Black Forest Gateau'

Alva: 'Victoria Sponge'

Renata: 'Lemon Meringue'

Alva: 'Madeira'

Renata: 'Battenburg'

Alva: 'Sticky Toffee Pudding'

Renata: 'Angel Food Cake'

Alva: 'Bakewell'

Renata: 'Tiramisu'

And on and on and on. Really silly, and laughing at us and half showing-off too.

Finally Anna shouted, 'Shut *up*! We just want to make a

six-year-old's birthday cake!'

Renata got down a cookery book, opened it and said, 'There!'

It was a photo of a big chocolate cake with smarties and cream splotches on top.

Anna said, 'So how do we make it?'

Renata said, 'Follow the recipe, stoopid.'

Then she and Alva trailed out. As she was leaving Alva said kindly, 'Beat the mix. Always beat the mix more than you think you need to.'

So we only got one tip and it wasn't enough ... When the cake came out of the oven, everyone was back in the kitchen except Anna's dad. The cake had sunk. It looked like deflated balloon, all sad and sagging. A big silence greeted our cake. Then Tommy began to laugh. And that set Alva and Renata off in *hysterics*. Anna pushed her lip out ...

Anna's mum said, 'Renata!' and then, 'It will be fine when you've iced it and put on the cream and smarties, you'll see. I'm sure it *tastes* delicious.'

'It would want to,' said Renata.

'You didn't beat the mix enough,' said Alva, 'I *told* you to beat the mix more than you think you need to.'

'People who say "I told you so" should be shot,' said Anna.

SATURDAY OCTOBER 3RD

Back from party. Oh my God! Gonna go play in the traffic ...

SUNDAY OCTOBER 4TH

OK. Have recovered from yesterday. I am now supposed to be doing my homework before Sunday dinner. Instead I will write all about the party:

So, we arrived at Mrs Mahony's in good time, with everything made – the rice crispy buns and the sandwiches and the cake and the Going Home Bags. Mum gave us a lift, and she walked us to the door to help carry the stuff. The door opened before we'd rung the bell, and there was a supermodel.

Well, a mini-supermodel. She was only a kid, but she had a supermodel body (long skinny legs and arms), and supermodel hair (poker straight with a half-fringe over the eyes), supermodel clothes (leggings and ballet pumps and short smock dress), and supermodel eyes – enormous in a very small face. *Flick*, she tossed her head to the left so her fringe lifted up and came back down over her eyes.

'Let's see my cake!'

I looked at Anna, then back at the supermodel, 'You're *Chloe*?'

'Uh-huh … let's see my cake.'

Mum began to laugh and said, 'Let's bring everything in.'

So we all went through to the kitchen.

I muttered to Anna, 'It's a baby supermodel.'

She hissed back, 'No. A proper supermodel. They're signing

55

them up young.'

Then we began to giggle. I thought it was in fact very possible that they were signing up six-year-old supermodels, seeing as a) six-year-olds are very skinny, b) they have perfect skin and c) they are good at smiling naturally for the camera.

Chloe looked at the cake. We had iced it that morning and put cream and smarties on it. But nothing could hide the dip in the middle, and the cream just made it look … *messier*, because cream is not very *neat* looking.

When Renata saw it iced and creamed, she said, 'That is the kind of cake that causes food fights. You just wanna pick it up and push it – *splotch!* – into someone's face …'

And she'd looked longingly at the cake and at my face, so I'd taken firm hold of the plate, because she would have, she absolutely would have – and '*Oh, Renata!*' is all she'd have got for doing it.

But the thing is that the cake looked even *worse* under Chloe's gaze than it did in Anna's kitchen. It looked like it was hanging its head in shame. I got ready for Chloe's sneer. But it never came. Instead her eyes filled with tears. Very slowly. Nothing else in her face changed – her skin didn't go blotchy, her mouth didn't tremble, none of the usual signs of crying. Just her big eyes welled up. Supermodel tears.

Anna said impatiently, 'Look, if you wanted a designer cake, your mum should have ordered one, not got us to *make* it.'

The tears began to slowly slide down the face, quiver on the chin, then drop to the ballet pumps. I watched fascinated. But I felt sorry for Chloe. Anna didn't, I knew. She hates girlie girls. Also I was worried Chloe's mum was about to come in and we'd have a disaster on our hands, so I gave Chloe a hug.

'It's cool. Wait until we put the candles on. It'll look great. Anyway it's *home-made*. That means it tastes great. Taste is more important than looks.'

'It is?'

'Of course!'

Chloe was only six after all, even if she did look like a super-model, so she was ready to be persuaded. We got out the candles and put them round and then we put the fat Number 6 in the centre. The cake now looked like a big, messy child's painting covered in stickers. Or like a teddy left out in the rain with its white stuffing coming through torn stitches. I made sure not to look at Anna. We would have had hysterics.

'See?' I said brightly. Chloe looked very unsure.

'And wait until the candles are lit,' said Anna, 'And wait until you taste it.'

The birthday girl began to smile, very uncertainly. It was just a little supermodel upturn of the lips. I quickly grabbed the cake and put it on top of a cupboard.

'Keep it a surprise till later,' I said. Just in time because Mrs Mahony came into the kitchen with a little boy. I didn't want to

have to go through the cake fiasco with her yet. Guess she's harder to persuade than a six-year-old.

Anna said importantly that we wouldn't put any food out till after the games otherwise the kids would just eat it. She sounded like a pro. I was very impressed at this clever method of postponing the Cake Fiasco.

Then Chloe said, 'Did you bring me a present?'

The little boy turned his eyes on us too.

'And me?'

He was about four. He looked like a squashed football, not like a supermodel, bad luck for him!

Mrs Mahony said, 'Oh Chloe, they're here to organise your party. I *told* you! Not to bring you presents. And Jake, it's Chloe's birthday, not yours – *she's* getting the presents.'

So I took a look at Chloe and sure enough the big eyes which had just emptied were beginning to fill up with tears all over again. Then I heard a nasty squawk like a cat makes if you tread on its paw, and it was Jake. He was screeching. The *exact* opposite to his sister's silent tears. Maybe he was adopted? Maybe Mrs Mahony changed husbands in between children? Where was Mr Mahony anyway?

Anna said quickly, 'Let's go hide sweets in the garden before everyone comes!'

In the garden – as we directed Chloe to put the sweets in the flower beds and Mrs Mahony totally contradicted us by

directing Chloe not to go *near* the flower beds – I sidled up to Anna, 'The Birthday Girl is a bit weepy ...'

'That's why her eyes are so big. She bulks them out with water ...'

'Take a bet on how many times she weeps today?'

'Twenty,' said Anna, 'Twenty euro on twenty times.'

Well, this was a good estimate! Because Chloe's eyes filled up when:

1) 3pm. None of her friends have arrived: 'They're not coming ...'

2) 3.17pm. She opens a present of a book: 'I've already got a book.' ('It's okay,' says Anna soothingly, 'books are like dresses, you can have more than one.' – 'You can?' – 'Yes, look, they all have different covers ...')

3) 3.33pm. Chloe is rushing round grabbing all the sweets in the garden. She knows where they are because she helped hide them. I suggest, very *very* gently: 'Maybe you should let your guests find some sweets ...'

4) 3.36pm. Not Chloe's tears this time. Her mother's: 'They're *ruining* the flower beds.' Her eyes, though not big and supermodelly like Chloe's, definitely look a bit weepy. Anna calls off the sweet-hunt.

5) 3.45pm. Pass the Parcel. The parcel doesn't land on Chloe ...

6) 3.55pm. Musical Statues. Chloe moves. Everyone sees her move ...

7) 4.10pm. Musical Chairs. Chloe misses the chair … ☹

8) 4.18pm. Pin the Tail on the Donkey. Chloe pins it on his ear … ☹

9) 4.20pm. Aleesha pins the tail, bang, on the donkey's bum. Aleesha also won the Parcel and Musical Statues. Aleesha is an adorable girl with red pigtails and red freckles like Pippi Longstocking. Suspect Anna cheated to help her win the parcel. Chloe: 'She *wins every*thing!' ☹

10) 4.30pm. Chloe wins Musical Statues Mark 2. Musical Statues Mark 2 hastily improvised because we had no games left, but Chloe needs to win a prize (Mrs Mahony says so). In Musical Statues Mark 2, the prize is for the Most Interesting Statue. Aleesha contorts herself into a hideous and Most Interesting Statue like a Troll. Chloe stands straight and vacant like supermodel on the end of the runway. Chloe gets the prize. Mutterings of discontent ('*her* statue wasn't interesting!' – 'yeah, it was *rubbish!*') No prizes left so we had to improvise a prize of some sweets which were left over from the hunt. Chloe not impressed with prize … ☹

11) 4.38pm. Tea-time! Chloe is elbowed off the head of the table by Karen. Karen has short, black hair and demands to be addressed as Carl. (Aleesha saves the day: 'It's Chloe's birthday, Karen, *she* has to sit at head of table!' All the other little girls: 'Yeah, Karen, it's *Chloe's* birthday!' Luckily, little girls are a) do-gooders and b) nerdy about rules). ☹

12) 4.54pm. Cake appears. Karen: 'That's a *rubbish* cake!' Chloe … 😠

13) 4.56pm. Bedlam! Something about our cake has unleashed the demons within the nerds. Karen started by digging her hand into cake and flipping a splotchy bit at Aleesha … Everyone froze. Then everyone went mad flinging cake! Except Chloe … 😠

14) 5.01pm. Food fight over. Order restored by yours truly and Mrs Mahony. Anna too helpless with laughter to restore order. Everyone singing 'Happy Birthday', but no cake left to sing it to. Cake all over the little girls. Chloe unappeasable. 😠

15) 5.15pm. Enter Mr Mahony. Chloe and little girls by now cleaned of cake and Playing Nicely – Anna has given them pieces of paper to draw their Ideal Cake on. Karen's Ideal Cake is just like ours – a splotchy sagging mess. Chloe sees her father – 'Daddy … … my cake …' Mr Mahony is tall and thin with enormous eyes behind glasses – obviously the source of the supermodel. He backs away from the room and his daughter's brimming eyes as if he's just witnessed a child being fed to a crocodile. 😠

16) 5.38pm. Last child gone home. Chloe: 'My party's o-o-o-over!' 😠

17) 5.42pm. No Going Home Bag for the Birthday Girl: 'Where's *my* Going Home Bag!' Anna: 'It's a *going* home bag,

you're not *going* home, you're *at* home!

18) 5.44pm. 'Where's *my* At Home Bag?'

19) 6pm. Me and Anna leaving. Chloe: 'Wouldn't you like to stay and play with my new toys?' Us: 'We can't, sorry.'

MONDAY OCTOBER 5TH

The party was worth it – not just for the money (not *even!*) but cause it's such a good story. Everybody is laughing about it. So now I know: Anna was right – these parties are good for a comedy blog. (N.B. Must get going on blog soon!)

David Leydon has started hanging out with Brian and Derek. This figures. Brian and Derek have attitude. They have long fringes, and listen to music which sounds like vomiting or cats screeching and they try hard not to try to be popular, and make like they consider the rest of us spoilt little rich kids, which is not very observant of them because Anna and I are definitely not spoilt or rich, but some others are, it's true (naming no names!) If you'd asked me and I'd thought about it I guess I'd have guessed David Leydon would hang out with them. Although he might have got friends with J.P. and he still might. Although, maybe he's too ... young? Uncool? ... for J.P. I mean I think he's cool till I compare him to J.P. and then I see he's more like the rest of us than he's like J.P.

J.P. is in our year but he's too cool for school. This is a stupid phrase, I admit, but it is the only possible phrase for J.P. so, sorry,

I have to use it. I *definitely* fancy J.P. and so does everybody else, it's just that nobody will admit it. This is because he's ugly and dirty – he doesn't even wash. He has long, lank, greasy hair and small red-rimmed eyes and white pasty skin and a big nose (Wow! Doesn't he sound dreamy?) There is something dangerous about him like he might suddenly do something crazy. He's also rude and jeering, although he's not cruel rude, I mean, it's good-tempered jeering. But what with him being dirty and ugly and dangerous and jeering, nobody can admit to fancying him. Tommy is the acceptable face to fancy cause he's good-looking and charming and artistic and kind-hearted, blah blah blah. But, fact is, when J.P. speaks to you, you get goosebumps and he has this way of looking at you ... Even Anna fancies J.P. (I know though she's never admitted it).

But anyway David Leydon hasn't graduated to J.P. yet. After break Anna had Spanish and I had French, so we separated and I saw David Leydon with Brian going towards French, so I caught up with them, and said 'Hi ...'

They said, 'Hi'.

I said to David, 'So did you stay long in town?'

He looked completely blank. This was potentially mortifying!

I said, 'Last Saturday..?'

'Oh yeah ... yeah... we hung round a bit...' Then he said 'How was your kid's party?'

It's incredible that he remembered this!

I said, 'Well, our cake caused a food fight, and the birthday girl cried *nineteen* times, and our games ruined the flower beds, but otherwise fine, perfect!'

Derek started to laugh, so the others did too. (I meant them to!).

Brian said, 'What were you doing at a kid's party?' but he has an inner city accent, so it sounded like, 'Wha' were you doin' a' a kid's par-ey.'

I started to tell him, but then we reached French class.

I have made contact and am cementing my friendship with David Leydon. Chloe's party is worth its weight in cake and tears!

Oh – we have decided what to do to Pierce we are going to hide his homework. This is Simple, but Effective.

TUESDAY OCTOBER 6TH

Today was The Day. We took Pierce's English homework. It was quite easy. At break we found his schoolbag by the lockers and took out his copybook and just ripped out the English essay. It was a spiral copybook so it didn't even show where we ripped. Then I put it carefully in my copybook so the pages would stay neat because today his homework was going to miraculously *disappear*, but tomorrow it had to miraculously *appear*, unharmed!

In Maths I took a quick look at Pierce's essay cause I was curious what he wrote. The essay was on *To Kill a Mockingbird* and

his first line was 'In my opinion Atticus Finch is one of the most important characters in Harper Lee's *To Kill a Mockingbird*.'

So I nudged Anna and whispered sarcastically, 'Guess what? Atticus Finch is one of the most important characters in *To Kill a Mockingbird*!'

'In Pierce's opinion,' said Anna, deadpan.

At the beginning of English class we all handed in our essays. I stole a look at Pierce. He was flicking through his copybook, front to back, back to front, front to back, with a totally amazed look on his face. He looked like someone had just plucked a Mars Bar out of his hands. All the essays were handed up. He didn't say anything. He didn't say anything right through the class, but just sat there. When the bell rang he went up to O'Toole. I lingered a bit going through the door and heard O'Toole saying, 'That's okay, Pierce, just bring it tomorrow.'

So now I know: Pierce is more cunning and diplomatic than Elaine. He stayed calm and totally got away with not having his homework. This proves that there is never any point losing your temper. It just makes things worse. I am surprised though. I would have thought he'd lose his temper and get all nasty.

'I think our Karma is a good test of character,' I told Anna, 'you get to see how people will react in a crisis. So now we know Pierce stays Cool, Calm and Collected.'

'Yeah,' said Anna, '*he'd* be good under fire.' Our history teacher, Mr McMahon, is big into battles and likes telling us

how we should behave if we're ever under attack, like this is likely to happen.

'And Elaine would be a rubbish,' I said, 'Hassled, Hysterical and …' I paused trying to think of a third H-word.

'Helpless,' said Anna, 'Hassled, Hysterical and Helpless.'

After lunch Anna and I crept into the boys' changing rooms and put Pierce's English essay back in his book. This was actually very brave of us. We'd be in real trouble if we were caught in the boys changing rooms. But we didn't want Pierce to have to write a whole new essay. That wouldn't have been fair, and the Instruments of Karma actually play it very fair. We slipped the essay back between the pages; he wouldn't know it was there till he opened the book to write a new essay this evening. Then we legged it out of the changing rooms. My heart was beating very fast. This is very exciting and dangerous work!

'I wish I could see his face when he finds it back there,' I said.

'Yep, we're messing with his head,' said Anna.

'Maybe we should have changed the first line for him though. Maybe we should have cut out "in my opinion". He's gonna get a rubbish mark with an opening like that.'

'We're teaching him a lesson,' said Anna, 'not teaching him a *lesson*.'

WEDNESDAY OCTOBER 7TH

It is going round the class that (maybe!) we hid Pierce's homework!

This morning Pierce was telling Ben, 'When I got home, it was just there! In the middle of the book, but I swear it wasn't there earlier.'

Ben kind of nodded but he wasn't too interested. It is hard to get interested about Unlikely Occurrences that happen to other people.

Then Anna butted in, 'Did you get in trouble?'

Pierce said, 'O'Toole let me off if I brought it in today, but he said not to let it happen again, like two strikes and I'm out.'

'Yeah,' said Anna, 'it's rough getting penalised when it isn't your fault.'

That's all she said, but Pierce suddenly looked closer at her. And by first break the whisper was going round that we'd hidden his homework. Then he confronted us with it.

He stood in front of us, with Ben, and said, 'Did you steal my homework?'

Ben was looking a lot more interested about the whole thing then earlier.

So I said, 'What are you talking about?' in a casual, impatient, bewildered voice, which was just exactly the right kind of voice. Maybe I should become an actress!

Ben said, 'Come on! You stole his homework to get him back for not paying you interest, didn't you?'

Anna said, 'That would have been a brilliant idea!' in a very enthusiastic voice, but like it had just occurred to her. Also very

convincing – she could be an actress too.

And I said, 'Huh! It's your guilty conscience for not paying like you *said* you would, that makes you think it's us.'

We went on like that, and they couldn't pin anything on us. They *suspected* us, maybe, but they weren't *sure*. We were so relaxed, they were *un*sure.

In the end I said, 'Do you really think we'd do that to *you*? I mean you'd *kill* us.' And I watched his face go all flattered and sly and could see him thinking to himself, 'Yeah, they'd be too scared to get *me*.'

Later Elaine said, 'It was you two, wasn't it?'

Anna said, 'It was Karma.'

Elaine said, 'Karma?'

I said, 'If you do something bad, it gets back to you, that's the Karmic circle.'

'What comes around goes around,' said Anna.

THURSDAY OCTOBER 8TH

We – me and Anna – have agreed it's quite good we're *suspected* of stealing Pierce's homework because it's kind of publicity for the Instruments of Karma. We can't advertise our services so we need the word to be whispered round. But at the same time we can't have people *knowing* it as a Sure Thing because we could get in trouble, so at first break we found Emma and swore her to secrecy about Elaine's gym-bag. Well, we kind of threatened her

to secrecy. We said if she told something bad would happen her. This was the only way to make sure she didn't blab. She hasn't said anything so far, but that's because she's afraid of admitting her part in it, but I bet that if the conversation got round to us and Pierce's homework, she'd start in on the gym-bag. Just because it would make a good story – she'd get everyone's attention, and normally she never gets *anyone's* attention. People will say anything to get everyone's attention, I've discovered. But I think we scared her bad enough for her to stay dumb. She's not so hard to scare. She's like jelly. We didn't mean the threats of course. That was just our excellent acting.

SATURDAY OCTOBER 10TH

No birthday party to organise today. I'm afraid that maybe the word has gone round the six-year-olds and their parents that we are Trouble. This is pretty unfair because actually if Mrs Mahony had been left to organise that party by herself she would have had a nervous breakdown and probably Karen would have ripped the Birthday Girl's dress and hacked off her supermodel hair.

MONDAY OCTOBER 12TH

Back in business! We have a party for next Saturday – a five-year-old boy's from the next road to Anna's. We dropped

cards in all the houses round hers and mine. This time we are gonna ask for €55 to buy food and prizes, and we don't do birthday cakes. Well, we will buy one, but not out of the €55. We are getting the hang of this.

Oh and we're *finally* doing the blog! It's going to be a proper blog, like a website, not just a Facebook entry. We need a proper blog because a) we have too much to write just for Facebook, and b) in Facebook you have to follow a set formula and we need to express our creativity by not following a formula, and c) you go on Facebook to make friends and comment on everyone else's entries and our blog is for the whole world to read, not just signed-up friends.

Declan, this friend of Tommy's, is helping us design the blog. Declan is a computer genius and quite nerdy. He has glasses, and spots, and is bad at sport. Outside school, like in Anna's house, he wears just jumpers and cords. He is not exactly the friend you'd expect for Tommy because he's not cool at all, but in fact him and Tommy are good friends. Maybe because of music; Declan is not in a band like Tommy, but he makes electronic music.

Anyway, how he agreed to help us design the blog was he was in Anna's kitchen with Tommy, when I said to Anna, 'We've got to get going on our blog!' and she said, 'Yeah, I know …', but not in that interested a way.

She is not as interested in this as me, and also she was drawing

with Charlie so wasn't really concentrating.

But Declan said, 'Your blog?' immediately interested, because it was to do with computers, so I told him my idea and he and Tommy cracked up laughing in a definitely patronising, but also a cheerful way, if you know what I mean.

Declan said, 'So what adventures are you putting in?'

I said, 'Adventures like the birthday parties. Funny adventures!' Then I explained about The Party People. I didn't go into the Instruments of Karma.

Tommy said, 'It's not exactly "from the war zone", is it? Not exactly "Adolescent life from besieged Baghdad" or "Under the Veil: teenage girls speak out from Iran".' He was really taking the piss now, bit like Renata, but less cutting.

I sighed because actually I am quite jealous of teenagers in war zones and dictatorships because everyone wants to read their blogs. But I said, 'Write what you know. All experience is relevant!' in a deliberately prissy, teacher-y voice, because that's what O'Toole says when we have to write stories. He never wants us to imagine we're stolen by space aliens, or that we're international spies, or that we're witches or wizards. He always just wants us to write about our own lives. I dunno about this. I think it has led to some really boring stories. I mean, imagine Pierce's stories: 'I got up. I had breakfast. I watched TV.' I think it would be better getting him to imagine being an arch criminal. Even Mr O'Toole said once, 'These are dull, dull, *dull*!' and with every 'dull' he

whacked his palm down on our pile of stories. Every so often he gets enraged like this but unfortunately for him it's always more funny than scary, so it doesn't affect our behaviour much. But it's true that thanks to him I sometimes look at my life and see which bits of it would work in a story. And sometimes I get to thinking what situations mean, why did someone do that, what is the story behind the story? And now I think about it, if Pierce actually told the *truth* about his life – I mean if he wrote about bullying people, then this would a) make a more interesting story (nasty-interesting but still *interesting)* and b) might make him think about why he's doing it. Still he never would. O'Toole wants us to tell the truth in our stories. But that is way ambitious of him. You're not going to tell the truth in a story that the whole class might read. Just in a diary (*ha!*)

Anyway, Tommy and Declan got my 'Write what you know. All experience is relevant' immediately because that's O'Toole's famous catchphrase.

Declan said, 'Yeah, Tommy, they could be like Sami.'

Tommy laughed.

I said, 'Who's Sami?'

Turns out Sami is a Turkish blogger who got an astronomical number of hits. He is a cult, and all because his blog is so boring. All he does is write about what he has for tea and what his mother-in-law says and things like that. I thought this was a pretty insulting comparison because our adventures are better

than *that* but anyway I laughed to show I was a good sport. And then Declan said, well, if we were really set on it, he'd help us design the blog! I gasped. This is incredibly kind of him!

THURSDAY OCTOBER 15TH

Another Karmic duty! Maybe the whispering campaign worked in our favour because at break Gita came up to us and she isn't even in our class. She's a First Year, like Justine. So our reputation is spreading! She is the daughter of someone in the Indian Embassy. Our school gets a lot of embassy kids, I don't know why because it's not top of the league for Leaving Cert results or anything. Maybe it's because our school is mixed boys and girls, when most secondary schools are single-sex. Even though we wear uniforms, our school looks a bit more like a school on American TV than other schools in Dublin. We can wear jewellery and boys can have long hair and sometimes you see kids kissing. Maybe embassy kids want their schools to be as close to America as possible? Anyway, Gita said would we do something bad to Jayne O'Keeffe because she was saying racist things to her. Anna went nuts over this! There is nothing worse than racism for a person with a strong social conscience.

FRIDAY OCTOBER 16ᴴ

Declan said to check out as many blogs as possible and see which

ones we liked the look of and then he'd help us design it. Thanks to Declan we're gonna have a really cool-looking blog that will avoid all the clichés. But I'm worried about how to blog about the Instruments of Karma because we can't really admit to it, but on the other hand it is too good *not* to put up. This is a Conundrum.

We are taking our job for Gita very seriously. In fact we considered not charging her because this is a question of Justice, but then Anna pointed out that Robin Hood stole from the rich to give to the to poor but Gita isn't the poor – no way, she wears designer shoes. To school! So we are charging her €10.50. We haven't decided what to do yet. It is a very serious crime that Jayne is committing and we think this time she needs to know why she's being punished. For something as serious as *racism* it's not enough to leave it to Karma.

SATURDAY OCTOBER 17TH

Back from Conor's – he is the five-year-old whose birthday we organised. Now I can say with complete assurance that little boys are much easier and nicer than little girls. Little boys – at least little boys of five – don't like being dumped by their parents. They are mad clingy! So there were all these parents chatting with us trying to organise games and nobody was too bothered about anything. If a little boy started acting up all you had to do was speak in a stern voice, and he would totally collapse and

promise to be good. Amazing! I am worried about these little boys in school though – they must be bossed to bits by the little girls.

Anyway it's good that the party was easy because we are not nearly as exhausted as last time, but it's also bad because there's no good story for the blog. I think I would rather be wrecked. I really would. I am ready to make this sacrifice for the blog.

SUNDAY OCTOBER 18TH

Anna came round to mine and we worked out what we were gonna post on our blog. She insisted on doing it in my house because she said if we did it in hers everyone would get involved and Renata would rewrite it. This is undoubtedly true.

We looked up loads of blogs to get ideas.

Anna said, 'You need loads of photos.'

'Yeah, and not too much writing,' I said.

'Yeah, and a kind of a *babyish* style' said Anna.

'Yeah, a kind of an exclamation mark style!' I said, because it's true, lots of blogs seem to be written like eight-year-olds exclaiming.

'*Not* in O'Toole-approved style!' said Anna. We were ages uploading it, and we had loads of fights about it, but we also had hysterics laughing. So this is what we ended up with:

I'm Bomb

[photo of Anna with a hat coming down over her face so you

can't recognise her]

and I'm Demise

[photo of me bending down with my head between my legs so all you can see is my back and hair. This a) hides my face and b) shows how bendy I am. I am extremely naturally bendy. For instance, if I sit down cross-legged I can suck my toes!]

Bombs cause demises so I'm the boss of *her*.

[photo of Anna sitting on my shoulders – only showing our backs.]

We like:

Music!

[photo of our CD collections – pride of place, *Kanye West* and *Lady Gaga* (me); *Daft Punk* and *The Doors* (Anna) She is highly influenced by Tommy and John so she likes really old music by people who died really young.]

Books!

[photo of our books – pride of place, *To Kill a Mockingbird* and *His Dark Materials* (me), *Crime and Punishment* (Anna)]

We are interested in:

Saving the environment!

[picture of cows, and underneath this caption:

'Did you know that cows' farts release meth-ane gas that damages the ozone!? What do YOU think should be done about this?']

Fighting injustice!

[We don't have a photo for this yet. Anna thinks we should

put up a photo of Pierce looking nasty, but I think this could be
A Step Too Far]

The animals we most resemble are:

[photo of a chipmunk and arrow saying:

Bomb!

Photo of a frog and arrow saying:

Demise!

It is quite hard to admit we look like a chipmunk and a frog.
We would rather look like a stallion or an Irish wolfhound
(Anna), or a black panther or an ocelot (me). But the sad truth is
we could not look less like a stallion or a black panther. Guess
who decided which animals we looked like? Yep, you got it,
Renata. We were wondering about it in Anna's kitchen one day,
after reading *His Dark Materials*. We were saying what would
our daemon be. (This is the same as saying what animal do I look
like).

Renata suddenly went off into her horrible cackle of laughter
over all our suggestions, and then she said, '*You* (pointing at
Anna) look like a chipmunk, and *you* (pointing at me) look like a
frog.'

'Chipmunk!' – 'Frog!' we howled.

Renata gave her evil, sparkly smile, 'Yes, you are small and dark
and you're always collecting, *amassing*, things, but you've got a
dirty temper and you *bite*, just like a chipmunk, and *you* have
googly eyes and skinny arms and legs and you can't keep *still*.'

We waited, and 'Oh, Renata!' said her mother.

But after a bit Anna said, well chipmunks are cute, and I said, well frogs are really bendy, they can do the splits! And since then we have become attached to our animals.

We are in business:
Organising children's parties!

[lots of photos from Conor's party yesterday that we took]

Now read our weekly blog!

[account of Supermodel's birthday party, quite like account I already wrote so I don't need to repeat it here]

We don't use loads of exclamation marks!!!! and question marks????? because we think they look stupid. And we're not writing in text-speak like, 'u r 4real & u r gr8' cause we hate text-speak. We considered writing the whole blog in predictive text, but it seemed like too much hard work for our readers.

Anna says we have to at least try to keep this blog a secret from people, especially our parents, because, she says, the blog isn't a notice board. I agree!

But I said, 'Tommy knows …'

She said it was okay for *Tommy* to know. He wouldn't tell. Tommy is her favourite person in her family. Probably her favourite person in the world. Well, no, it is a toss-up between him and Charlie, I guess, but Charlie is only two, so he can't

really be a favourite *person*. He is more like a puppy-dog.

Still haven't thought what to do to Jayne O'Keeffe yet.

MONDAY OCTOBER 19TH

Went to Anna's after school to work with Declan on our blog. Not in the kitchen, of course. In Tommy's bedroom. Declan and Tommy actually laughed at what we'd put up! Me and Anna exchanged glances and squirmed with excitement because they are our first audience, and they found it funny.

Tommy said, 'Very funny.'

I said, 'Yeah, well, we were copying the other blogs.'

Declan said, 'That's obvious. You've been copying blogs by people who can't speak English.' He laughed.

I looked at Anna, a bit embarrassed. *Now* we knew why they all wrote like eight-year-olds exclaiming! Maybe this wasn't cool? But Tommy said, 'It's cool. Look, it's better than coming across all earnest.'

'Oh yeah,' said Declan 'it's hysterical.' But then he looked at the photos of the party, 'I'm not sure you can show these,' he said 'not without permission. I'm pretty sure you can't just put photos of other people's kids on the web.'

We were disappointed about this. But Declan had a look at some of the photos and said he'd photoshop them. He's gonna blur out the kids' faces and blow up the birthday cake, cause apparently you're allowed to show other people's kids' birthday

cakes on the web. But he said next time to take photos without kids, or just with bits of kids, a leg would be okay, or a little hand reaching for cake, because all kids' legs and hands look the same.

Then Declan started playing round with the design – changing the background colour and moving round the photos and asking did we like the letters this size? Or like this? Or this? To be honest I couldn't see much difference, they seemed small unimportant changes, and his questions were giving me a headache.

We went back down to the kitchen and Anna's mum asked if I wanted to stay to dinner. Which was great! So I phoned Mum to ask and she said no! I couldn't believe it.

I said, 'But Mum …' and she said, 'No, Denise, we want you home for dinner.' And I couldn't start arguing over the phone in Anna's house, so I had to just say 'okay' and hang up, and then explain in as normal voice as I could that I wasn't allowed. I don't know how normal my voice was though, because I was raging.

But Anna's mum said, 'Well, it's a school night, I do see your mother's point.' She has a very soothing voice. Maybe this is because of her job. She has to talk to mad people. Probably they need soothing.

When I got home I said, 'How come I couldn't stay for dinner?' in a quite reasonable voice, I thought, but Mum said, 'I'm not starting a fight over this, Denise. You spend quite enough time in Anna's. I'm not having them feed you as well.'

I thought that was crazy. 'They don't mind,' I said.

'Well, *I* mind,' she said.

I had a good answer to that. I was gonna say, 'It's not about *you*,' because it wasn't, but before I could get this out Dad said, 'That's enough now, lay the table,' in a warning voice and I decided to swallow my words instead of having a big old row and being sent to my room and not getting fed.

They are definitely stifling my freedom of speech and I am letting them.

I decided the only way to get back at them without getting into trouble was to sulk and not speak through dinner. I wanted to point out that we were just eating boring old chicken while at Anna's they were having an exciting *pink* soup called boar-shsh or something like that, but I managed not to comment on what we were eating, and not to say anything in fact. I didn't even make an issue of it when Justine got *both* the wings.

I *commented* on it obviously, I said 'Hey, why is she getting both?'

But when Mum said, 'Oh, don't be such a baby, they're her favourite,' I kept my mouth shut, although it wasn't *me* being the baby and the wings were wasted on Justine. She doesn't know how to pick bones clean and she didn't even eat the skin! It was a very quiet meal. Dad is the quiet type and recently he's just been exhausted from work, and Justine never says anything, of course. I realised then that it is only me and Mum keeping this family talking.

TUESDAY OCTOBER 20TH

Here's what we're gonna do to Jayne: we are gonna get loads of stickers and write *Racist!* on them and stick them to her back, her bag, her locker, etc.

This is definitely the most daring, bravest thing we've done yet as Instruments of Karma but the punishment must fit the crime and the crime is serious!

I said we'd better run it by Gita. Anna said, why bother? Because, I told her, if she *doesn't* agree to it *initially*, she might use it *later* as a way to get out of paying. She might say: *that's not what I meant, I'm not paying.* Anna was pretty impressed by this argument. So was I – it sounded just like something an economist would say.

Actually Gita thought it was a brilliant idea, but she was nervous too.

'Jayne's gonna think it was me,' she said. She was getting in a state about it.

Anna said, 'Well what do you want us to do?' quite belligerently.

But then Gita calmed down, 'I know, I'll be off sick that day. You gonna do it tomorrow? Day after? Okay, I'll be off sick. Then she can't blame me!' This seemed pretty neat, but pretty cowardly too!

'If you're off sick, you'll miss her reaction,' said Anna, but we left it at that.

WEDNESDAY OCTOBER 21ST

After school we stopped off and brought a roll of plain white stickers, not too big, but big enough and some markers and then we went to Anna's and straight up to her room to design the stickers. This was definitely not something to do in the kitchen! On most of the stickers we wrote: Racist! in big black jagged letters like this: **RACIST!** (Anna) and **RACIST!** (me) and we coloured in the background red. But some of them we did in red on a green background, and some in black on a yellow background. Anyway, they all looked very noticeable and truly alarming.

THURSDAY OCTOBER 22ND

We placed the first stickers just before first class. We put a black and yellow one and a black and red one on Jayne's locker. At break she obviously hadn't been to her locker yet because we saw her in the playground chatting quite normally. Then we had to do a very tricky and difficult manoeuvre. We had to get the sticker on her back without anyone noticing us. So we waited till everyone was filing back into class because then there's this big crush of lines and queues, and we got in behind her. We kept chatting very naturally to each other and Anna had the sticker in her hand and just lightly, lightly, very very lightly, she pressed it on Jayne's back so she couldn't feel it. And we didn't immediately disappear. We kept right on chatting to each other and

blocking everyone else's view of Jayne's back, until the last minute. We went right up the steps and into the corridor behind her, and then we just turned nonchalantly up the stairs. We totally got away with it.

At lunchtime we noticed these huddles of people from Gita's class standing round hissing in excitement about something. So we got up close to try and listen. We couldn't really make anything out, except 'Did you see?' and we didn't want to make ourselves conspicuous, so we moved off. It seemed pretty clear though. We went to look for Jayne. We couldn't see her anywhere, so we went inside. We passed by her locker and the stickers had been peeled off! A little bit of them was left on but not that you could make anything out. It looked like someone had used hot water. We stuck two more on. It was a pity we didn't know which was her gym bag to stick that too. Then the bell rang to go back to class.

FRiDAY OCTOBER 23RD

We weren't sure whether to keep up our sticker campaign – well, we needed to know how it was going. So at break we went to find Gita. She saw us coming and left her friends and came over.

'So?' we said. 'So she's not at school today,' said Gita, sounding really satisfied, 'and yesterday she was in tears apparently!'

I said, 'Wow!' but I thought: *in tears …!!*

'Everyone's talking about who did it,' said Gita, 'but of course

I'm not a suspect cause I wasn't even in school.' She sounded really proud, like she'd just got through stage six of *Tomb Raider* or something.

'Bully for you,' said Anna sarcastically. Then Gita gave us €11 and we gave her back 50 cent. 'So don't tell anyone it was us,' said Anna sternly in a quietly menacing voice.

'No way,' said Gita, 'that would get *me* in trouble!' She walked off. We looked after her.

'Well we're safe from *her* telling,' I said.

'For the moment,' said Anna, 'If she's suspected and questioned, she'll squeal. She'd sell her baby brother to save her skin.' I sniggered, and thought what a cute example – I mean the *worst* thing Anna could think of anyone doing is selling their baby brother. That is not the worst thing I can think of, but then I don't have a baby brother, it's true, just a little sister, who is not a baby any more.

We walked on.

'Didn't know Jayne would *cry*,' I ventured, 'and not coming into school today... well...'

'Serve her right,' said Anna, 'anyway, shows she's got a guilty conscience.' She sounded brash. She generally sounds brash, Anna, but she didn't sound 100 per cent brash.

SATURDAY OCTOBER 24TH

Declan told Tommy to tell us he'd done stuff to the blog, so

today at my house we took a look. (We couldn't do it at Anna's cause they'd be no privacy, and we don't necessarily want everyone knowing about this). It does look better. It's got a gorgeous green background colour, and the pictures of the party look funny, especially the close-up of the cake. If I came across this blog, I'd honestly think it was really entertaining and I'd want to know the girls who set it up. We don't come across as trying to seem sweet, cool or sexy, and that's the main thing.

What bonded me and Anna when we were first making friends at the beginning of First Year was how embarrassing people's web profiles were. Even people trying to seem ultra-casual always reveal themselves as trying too hard to project a certain image. Like Caroline Hunter putting up that baby picture, pretending she found it an *embarrassing* baby picture, because it showed her mouth all smeared with chocolate, but you just *knew* that she thought it was adorable and that she wanted everyone else to think it was adorable too. Or Celine putting up a picture of herself with backcombed hair and loads of black eye make-up and black lips, and underneath the caption: 'Marilyn Manson meets Dracula!' Well she was hoping by her ironic caption to dissociate herself from the photo, but she couldn't hide that she'd put it up because she thought she looked cool. And the thing is: she did look cool! Celine is very sexy because of being half French – she is super-skinny, and she always looks sulky, and she looks very cool when she smokes, unlike everyone else who look like

idiots when they smoke, which is part of the reason Anna and I don't smoke. (And also because it's bad for our health, and also because it's a ruinous habit, Anna says, meaning it's ruinously expensive. She knows this because her brother, John, at Oxford, smokes and he says there's no point starting because then you're hooked and before you know it, it's costing you €50 a week. €50 a week is *definitely* a lot of money! It is the profit from one and a bit children's parties! This Puts Things in Perspective, as Anna's mum says, and probably we will never smoke, although – who knows? – when we start college, it might just happen. At college people sit around and drink black coffee and smoke and go on marches protesting about what the Americans do to poor people.)

Anyway, so Celine really suits back-combed hair, and black eye-make up and black lips. It is A Good Look for her, and I could see why she wanted to put up that photo, and I don't know if I'd have been able to resist myself if I'd had such a good photo, but Anna said sternly, no way, you have to exercise control, and that it diminished Celine, and she was right, it did diminish Celine! It would have been okay if someone *else* had put up that photo – like if someone was putting up photos of a party, and that photo happened to be among them, but it is not okay to put up a flattering photo of yourself. That is the rule! Now that we know Celine is trying so hard to be cool, she is *less* cool.

Mum and Dad were out (at a garden centre probably! They

are obsessed with boring things like garden centres), but Justine wandered into the study while we were looking, probably 'cause she heard us having hysterics laughing, so I said 'Out, out!' and then, 'cause Anna kind of looked at me, I added, 'I'm sorry, but it's private,' in quite a nice voice. She left.

Then Anna said, 'We *could* let her into the secret.'

I said, 'Don't trust her.' That was not entirely true. I mean Justine hardly speaks. Who was she going to tell? She might tell someone in her class though, and then it would get round. Anyway I didn't want her knowing! Things are no fun when your family knows.

Afterwards we went round to Anna's cause Declan was there and we wanted to thank him. It's pretty amazing he did this for us. He is in fourth year! It's amazing he'd bother.

But he said, 'It's cool. I like doing those things.'

It's true he's a computer wizard, and probably he needs to practise. Probably he is going to invent something like Bill Gates did and he needs to get experience. Which means that actually *we're* doing *him* a favour! This is a good way of looking at it. He said he'd show us all the tricks of Photoshop in case we got more photos from kids' parties, and also he said he's not 100 per cent happy about the design, there are a few things he'd like to change, but he wants us to sign-off on them. So he said why not meet in town tomorrow and we'd go through it. He said to meet in Ukiyo because it's got wi-fi.

We said sure. He's taking a lot of trouble with us! I dunno why we're not just meeting in Anna's, but it's true we have to keep going up to Tommy's bedroom because of not wanting the rest of the family to know, and Tommy's bedroom is not the tidiest. There is another bed in it where John used to sleep, and still does sleep when he's home, but you can't hardly see it's a bed anymore, it is so overloaded with clothes and books and DVDs and CDs and crisp packets and chewing gum packets too (those are pretty gross!) Actually, there is nowhere to sit really. You have to try and find space on the bed by shoving up all the stuff on it. Well, maybe there is nothing you can do about boys' mess? Also Anna's mum believes in self-expression. Once Charlie began to draw on the wall with his crayons, so I screamed, 'Oh my God!' and she just said, 'Well, he needs to express himself. We mustn't inhibit him.'

I guess I looked shocked because she added, 'It will wash off. They're washable crayons.' So I wonder would he be allowed express himself in oil paints (ha!) Anyway, maybe Tommy's incredibly messy room is his form of self-expression?

What does 'sign-off' mean? And where is Ukiyo?

SUNDAY OCTOBER 25TH

So now we know an awful lot about web design. The thing is, well ... it's quite embarrassing. So, you're supposed to admit embarrassing things in your diary, right? That is what makes it

different to your blog, right? Well, so … on the way to meet Declan (we were sitting on the top of the bus on the front seat, which is the best seat in the bus), Anna goes, 'So, Declan must fancy you…'

I said, 'No way!'

She said, 'So why is he doing all this for us, then?'

'Cause he needs to practise computer programming, so he can grow up to be Bill Gates.'

'This isn't computer *programming*! This is easy. It's not *practice*. It's like … autopilot. Nah, he must fancy you.'

'Maybe he fancies *you*, so.'

'He's round ours all the time. He's been round ours for *years*. He's known me since I was ten. No way does he fancy me. If he fancied me, I'd know. And anyway you don't fancy people you've known since you were *ten*.'

'Well you might,' I said. 'In *Fire and Hemlock*, she meets Tom when she's ten, and he's at least *twenty*.' (*Fire and Hemlock* is this really good book by Diana Wynne Jones.) Anna paused to consider this; she couldn't deny it, but she came right back with her answer. She always does come right back.

She said, 'Yeah, but he doesn't fancy her *until* she's grown-up. I mean you might meet someone when they're ten, and then not see them for a long time, and then meet them when they're grown-up and fancy them. That *might* happen. But you don't just *suddenly* start to fancy someone when you're calling into

their house all the time.'

I couldn't comment because she knows more about this stuff then me. She has all these older brothers and sisters. She's been observing how people fancy each other for years.

I said crossly, 'Whatever. He couldn't fancy me. He's too old. Fourth years don't fancy second years!'

'They do too,' said Anna, sounding a hundred per cent sure, 'especially when they're nerdy like Declan, that's *exactly* who they do fancy, younger girls, who are sweet and unthreatening,' and she looked out the window and sang, 'That's why he picked you-oo ...'

So I thumped my fist down hard on her knee and said, 'I'll show you unthreatening' and she said, 'Ooh, he'd love it if you did that to him!' So I squealed quickly to banish the image of thumping Declan and him enjoying it, and thumped her *harder* and she thumped back and soon we were in one of our mad, giggly moods when everything is funny (to us, that is – it's never funny to anyone else).

Unfortunately for Declan this mood continued when we got off the bus and walked round Trinity College and across Grafton Street and into Ukiyo, which is this cool Japanese-looking café with low tables and not too much light. It's a place for grown-ups, I don't know why Declan wanted to meet here. Well, probably because it's a comfortable place to sit. There he was in the corner crouched over his laptop.

'Go and give him a quick thump,' whispered Anna, 'go on – make his day.'

I gave her a secret thump on the leg and then we were sniggering in front of Declan.

He hardly looked up. (Who says he fancies me?) He just said, 'Hi, sit down ...'

Anna said, 'You sit there, Denise,' meaningfully, pointing to the place beside him so I'd no choice, but I leaned right forward on the bench so that no bit of me was touching him.

We peered into Declan's laptop, which is so thin it looks like a large credit card. His mouse was whizzing round websites. Our PC at home is a lot slower.

Anna said dreamily, 'Wi-fi is like a dog with extra-sensory hearing. It picks up signals we can't.' (She loves dogs).

So I said, 'Woof-fi!'

She said, 'Woof-Fido!'

I said, 'Wi-Fi-Fo-Fum.'

I admit these jokes were very lame (I'm embarrassed just writing them down!), but we were in the kind of mood that thought they were hilarious. We kept on like that. Declan looked from one to the other, confused. Finally he managed to stop us being silly by showing us different ways to Photoshop. You can do a lot with photos if you know how. Declan said all photos in magazines are Photoshopped and the models don't actually look that good, which is good to know. We're not trying to improve our

looks though, we're just trying to crop kids' faces and enlarge their feet.

We were interested in Photoshop, but then Declan started in on the look of the blog. He wanted our opinion on miniscule changes to the background colours and I really couldn't see much difference between the hundred shades of green, and then he started on the letters, which he calls fonts, and did we want the font curly or slant, or bold or faint, or boiled or bubbled (well that's what it sounded like), and he started muttering names of font, like Arial and Verdana and Calibri and Palatino and Garamond and he was reminding me of Renata and Alva saying cake names, except his sounded like characters in Shakespeare, so I said, 'Titania would be good', and Anna got it immediately and said 'Bassanio' and I said 'Romeo' and she said 'Mercutio' and I said 'Caliban' and she said 'Bottom' and then we collapsed laughing.

Declan said, 'Oh, ha', in a confused way, although our names were as good as his. So then Anna tried to be polite and interested, but we were just feeling too silly and he was beginning to look quite desperate.

So Anna said, 'Oh, you decide Declan. Whatever you think – we don't mind, Titania or Oberon or Caliban, whichever you think looks best!'

I said, 'Yeah! And thanks', but I didn't thank him in the sincere, heartfelt way that I did the other day. I thanked him

in a rude, rushed, and offhand way.

This is what happens when you think someone who you don't fancy might fancy you. It makes you a) uncomfortable and rushed, b) rude and cruel. You feel quite powerful and then you start to exploit your power. Well *I* do. Apparently. Does this make me a nasty person? Probably.

So then we giggled our way in and out of shops. Some of the clothes shops were open. But I didn't feel like buying anything. I get quite confused about what to buy in clothes shops. Anna doesn't. She just wears jeans and t-shirts and runners. Everything she wears looks very clean and neat and cool and suits her. But she practically dresses like a boy. So do I, because it's easier. But I would like to wear wackier clothes. Actually I would like to dress like Renata in dresses over leggings and jumpers and belts and boots and bracelets. I am going to dress like that when I'm in sixth year.

When we were looking at bags in Topshop – Anna wanted this kind of canvas rucksack – Anna said, 'Do you think we ganged up on Declan?'

I said, 'We didn't mean to …'

She said, 'He was doing us a favour too.'

'You shouldn't have said he fancied me.'

'Yeah, well he does.'

'Maybe not any more … maybe he thinks we're annoying little girls.'

So then we began to giggle again. As we were coming out we bumped into Brian and his mum! We said, 'Hi, Brian', and he looked mortified like you'd expect because someone like Brian doesn't want to be seen with their mum, and he muttered, 'Hi …'

Then his mum said, 'Introduce me to your friends, Brian!' in a bossy voice.

Brian turned redder than ever and muttered, 'Anna, Denise,' and we said, 'Hi, Mrs Stewart!' in our best polite voices.

She kept us chatting a bit, but then we took pity on Brian and said we had to go.

'Bet she's giving out to Brian for not "introducing her nicely",' I said, and Anna said, 'Yeah … did you notice how posh her accent is?'

That was it! I knew there was something funny I couldn't put my finger on. She has a real D4 accent, what Renata calls 'strangled 4 by 4 vowels', and Brian, well, Brian sounds hard and rough.

No wonder he was so embarrassed meeting us! We have totally blown his cover. He is not a deprived inner city anarchist, he is a pampered little darling.

I said, 'Wow, we could so blackmail him.'

Anna said, 'Instruments of Karma don't blackmail,' in a very prim voice. I was only joking, obviously! The fact that she took it seriously means she is actually tempted to blackmail (I think!)

Well now I have to have dinner and then I have to think what to add to our blog.

Later

Have had a really good idea: I want to write all about Instruments of Karma on the blog, but I don't want it to get back to us and get us into trouble. So here's my cunning plan: I will report on what's happening in school, but not like I'm part of it. Instead I will just pretend to be an observer, as if I'm just any kid in the class saying what's going on. Well, I have to post something! It is not like we have enough kids' parties to fill up the blog.

Later again!

So here's what I wrote:

25th October

End of an exciting week at our school! Something funny is going on there. Last week someone stole X's homework. [X is the class bully!] We know it was stolen because one day it was gone, and the next day it reappeared. Like magic! I think whoever stole it was getting X back for being a bully.

This week someone stuck stickers saying RACIST! all over Y's coat, and bag, and locker. All over all her things, basically! Apparently

Y had said something racist to another girl, who is Indian. So whoever stuck those stickers up was showing her up. Maybe it's the same person who hid X's homework! Well who is it? I'll keep you posted!

Texted Anna:

Treated the clog. Take a look!

But she hasn't get back yet. Probably she is in bed. It is kind of late.

MONDAY OCTOBER 26TH

Today … well, today…

Shit!!! We're in trouble!

Well, *potential* trouble…

So we got into school to discover there was an assembly called for before first class. This is not usual. We don't have assembly except on very special occasions like first day of term, or when our debating team wins a big prize in Europe. So we were all pretty intrigued and excited. When we got to the hall we saw it was only a half special assembly – I mean only the lower school was assembled, First to Third Years. Right off you could see this was not a happy special assembly. The teachers had stern unmoved faces. Then Mr Lucas (our headmaster) came to the stage to address us. He looked VERY serious.

He said, 'A serious case of … bullying, or … *vendetta*, has taken place in the school.' Then he paused. A ripple moved through the classes, as everyone went *oooh* and turned to their friends. Me and Anna went *oooh* and turned to each other. Lucas went on, 'Some of you will know about this.' (pause) 'A student has been *branded*.' (long pause, he is a master of pauses!) My heart slowed right down … 'Yes,' said Lucas (I swear he was beginning to enjoy himself, I mean he had everyone's attention and he was *milking* it) 'someone in this room is playing *God*. Someone in this room is playing prosecutor, judge, and jury. Someone in this room has decided to condemn a fellow student as a racist and to anonymously brand her!'

The ripple swelled and almost burst. Lucas let it build. He gazed down on us. Everyone was exclaiming and turning. I didn't dare look at Anna. And then I thought: *not* looking at Anna is suspicious, *not* making noise is suspicious, so I turned to her and said, '*Whoa!*'

She was looking mutinous. Her face was fixed and stubborn like it is when Renata gets to her.

Lucas started speaking again, 'Perhaps the perpetrator acted with good intentions. Perhaps the perpetrator thought they were doing a good and a just thing. Perhaps the perpetrator thought they were striking a blow against racism. But we don't condemn people without a hearing in this school, or in this country. We don't decide unilaterally that someone is guilty. And we

certainly don't take anonymous revenge. Anonymity is the last refuge of the coward!' (He practically *shouted* that last sentence. And followed it up by another long impressive pause. He was definitely enjoying himself. He loves the sound of his own voice, and now that he had a good subject …) Then he lowered his voice to a more friendly tone, 'Racism is a very serious offence, one of the most serious offences we, in this school, ever have to deal with. If you suspect someone of racism, you mustn't ignore it, you *must* report it. But you *don't* take matters into your own hands! You *don't* apply *street* justice.' (Another long pause).

'"Vendetta" is a word from the Sicilian, it means "revenge", and it is what the mafia apply. Now you all know that the mafia are gangsters because you've all seen the movies.' (Pause for titter of laughter, which came of course, everyone sucking up to him … well I laughed too, sucking up for all I'm worth!) 'But what you perhaps *don't* know is that the mafia started off with good intentions. They felt there wasn't enough justice for the poor and they wanted to protect them. A bit like Robin Hood. So they took matters into their own hands. They dispensed justice. But justice can't be decided by a few. It is the business of courts. It has to be written into books. It has to be investigated, weighed up and discussed by experts – by police and lawyers and judges. And then it has to be dispensed in the open. Not anonymously! Not in the dark! Once you start doing that, things get underhand, they get corrupt, they get unfair, and before you know it, you

have a mafia!' (I looked at Anna, she rolled her eyes at me. Her look said: here we go, a history lesson *and* a moral lesson. Typical Lucas!) He was winding up now. 'In this school we teachers act as the court. You may think it's snitching to report things to us, but if someone is guilty of racism or of discriminating against their schoolmates they deserve to be snitched on.' (Pause) 'We are currently investigating the very serious charge. We may find that the person was judged unfairly, and did not deserve her branding. But regardless of the original offence, we take a very dim view of students carrying out vendettas. I have called this assembly to convey just what a dim view I take. We *will* find out whoever has done this, and they will have quite some explaining to do.' Pause for long final stare to make us feel he could see into our souls. Then quick turn on his heel and off he marched.

Consternation in assembly!

Now I know how a criminal feels: you have to *act* all the time. First we had to act really normal and discuss it naturally. We joined our class throng and said, 'What was that about?'

Caroline Hunter said importantly, 'It was Jayne O'Keeffe. Someone stuck stickers saying "Racist" on her coat and bag!'

'And now she's off school,' said someone else, 'she's in bits!'

'Well what racist thing did she do?' I said.

'Didn't you hear Lucas?' said Caroline, 'she didn't do *anything* racist. She got unfairly accused.'

'He didn't exactly say that,' said Elaine, 'he said they were

investigating it. I think she was racist to someone in her class.'

'No,' said Caroline, 'someone just wanted to get her into trouble by accusing her of the worst thing possible.'

'How do *you* know?' said Elaine rudely. Everyone starting joining in, saying what they thought, so we did too, acting surprised, interested, disbelieving, dumb ...

And as a criminal you feel paranoid. I felt everyone was looking at us, thinking: *they* did it. Because of the rumours about Pierce's homework, we might be suspects. No one said anything, but I was imagining them thinking it, and going to tell the teachers ... The only thing on our side was that Jayne O'Keeffe is not in our year.

But the worst thing about being a criminal is that you have to keep silent! You can't even discuss it with your accomplice. Everyone is watching you (or so it seems). Even at break me and Anna didn't dare discuss it. In fact we didn't dare go off alone. We hung round talking to other people instead. This didn't make any sense cause we're always going off alone, but suddenly it seemed that if we did people would say, *look at those two, what are they conspiring about?* And we certainly couldn't talk to Gita! That would have been like an admission of guilt.

So we had to wait till school was over to talk about it. And then we had to wait till we got off the bus (in case someone overheard) and were walking towards Anna's house. And then ... well we still could hardly discuss it. We didn't even want to look

at each other!

I said, 'What do you think?'

Anna said, 'If she was racist, she deserved it, the teachers wouldn't have done *anything*!' But she sounded not even half as sure as she usually does.

'But what if she *wasn't*? What if Gita was exaggerating?'

'She wouldn't ...' And then she trailed off, because the fact is, she *would*. Gita is just exactly the type of person who would exaggerate.

'Do you think they'll find out it's us?'

Anna said nastily, '*I'm* trying to think whether we did the right thing. I'm not worried about being found out. It's bigger than that!' She was getting all moralistic.

I said (also nastily, but undercover nasty), 'It would be better if we hadn't taken the money.' That was to get at her, cause she was the most interested in the money. And it's true: it would be kind of okay if we hadn't got paid for it. I didn't like to imagine Lucas' face if he knew we were paid for it!

'Let's ask your mum,' I said, 'we can ask in a *general* way, not admitting it was us ...'

'Yeah, ok,' said Anna. But her mum wasn't home. There was only Renata in the kitchen, eating yoghurt, and in a foul mood. And there was no point bringing it up with her. Who cared about her weird view on this? I left pretty quickly.

TUESDAY OCTOBER 27TH

Investigations are still going on in school over whether Jayne was racist or not. Someone said her parents came into school, and so did Gita's. So now everyone knows there was some incident between Jayne and Gita, and everyone is arguing over whether Jayne was racist or Gita was lying. The story is getting chewed up and mangled, at least in our class. No one knows what happened and everyone is taking sides. I had a lot of discussions about it. I have discovered another thing about being a criminal: you want to talk about the crime all the time.

When I got home I decided I'd ask Justine because it's her year. Justine might be quiet and boring, but she's good at noticing things and she always tells the truth, at least she did as a kid. She couldn't lie that was her problem, she'd turn bright red and her eyes would start bulging, and pretty soon she learnt just to own up quickly. So I brought up the whole incident at dinner, in a general way of course. I started telling my parents about it and Justine joined in, much more talkative than usual. I mean she was really interested in this.

I said, 'They're in your class. What do you think?'

She said, 'I don't *think* Jayne was racist ... I'd say she said mean stuff, but nothing actually racist. But Gita is new and Jayne is really mean to her. Jayne's mean to loads of people, but maybe Gita *thinks* it's because she's Indian. Or maybe Gita just wanted to get Jayne into trouble so she called her racist. Because

everyone knows that's the worse thing you can say in our school. But anyway, whatever, Jayne deserved it!'

I looked at Justine, quite surprised. She seemed in a bit of a state about this. And she sounded kind of vindictive, which is not like her. 'How did she deserve it?'

'Well, okay, maybe she didn't deserve to be called a racist' – Justine's voice gave full weight to the terrible accusation: *racist,* and I went all squirmy with guilt – 'but she's a horrible person. She makes people's lives a misery. So she deserved to see what it was like herself for once.'

I was glad to hear this, I can tell you. So she isn't actually racist, but she's a horrible person who deserved to see what it was like herself for once. So we hadn't been *too* unfair …

Mum said, 'Well – but where's the mystery? Surely this Gita is the prime suspect for the stickers then?'

'Yes, but she wasn't in school the day the stickers were put up,' said Justine importantly, 'so it couldn't have been her!'

'Now that *is* suspicious,' said Dad, 'suspiciously convenient. She must have put someone up to it.' He sounded amused. He thought this was funny! He only thinks things are funny about two times a year. He must be pretty smart, though, seeing as he worked out what happened.

'Yeah!' I said enthusiastically, cause I didn't want to look suspicious, 'that must be it. Bet she paid someone to do her dirty work.' (This was a very daring and clever thing to say. Diverted

suspicion by putting it out in the open!)

'Well the teachers will be on to her, I guess,' said Mum 'they'll have worked it out.'

'You think?' I said. My voice may have squeaked on the *think*. Squeaked with panic. Hope nobody noticed.

WEDNESDAY OCTOBER 28TH

Jayne is back in school. We saw her at break in an important huddle in the playground. Her friends were looking very protective and important because they knew everyone was looking. Some people were going out of their way to say hi to Jayne to show they didn't think she was a racist. But not everyone was. And she was looking a bit small and shrivelled. I don't know her but I've noticed her round. She's one of the First Years you notice. Normally she oozes popularity and bitchiness but she wasn't looking like that now.

'Justine said probably Jayne never said anything racist, but that anyway she's a horrible person,' I said.

Anna said in a snappy voice, 'You can't punish someone for one crime just because they're guilty of another – oh I'll put you in jail for murder cause I know you're guilty of theft!'

I snapped back, 'I didn't say you *could*. I just meant we didn't have to feel too sorry for her.'

Then we looked round for Gita. Not to *talk* to her – that would look way suspicious! – but just to see did she look worried.

But we couldn't see her anywhere.

'Maybe's *she's* off now,' said Anna.

At lunch I went to talk to Brian and Derek and David Leydon. Me and Anna thought we should separate and also we wanted to get away from each other. Well I did from her – because we only wanted to talk about one thing, and we couldn't talk about that at school, and all our jokes about other things have just gone.

I don't know whether I can say David Leydon is my friend. We talk, but it's me talking *at* him. He doesn't say much. But he doesn't walk off. Brian doesn't talk much either but that's probably because it's difficult for him to keep up his accent. If he spoke too long a sentence he might start sounding like his mum! The one who talks the most of the three is Derek. I'm discovering that under his long fringe and scruffy attitude, Derek is actually quite friendly. He's got these enthusiastic eyes, which somehow remind me of Justine's when she was small and wanted to join in my games. (Well his eyes are brown, not blue, like hers, and he doesn't look like a seven-year-old girl, but it's the same expression, like he's hoping there's fun round the corner and that I'll deliver that fun). I brought up the Racism Case (of course! I couldn't resist. It's like a pop-up. You know when you're on a computer and reminders keep popping up telling you to get more anti-virus or whatever? Well it's like that, whatever I'm doing or saying, the Racism Case keeps popping up, demanding attention). They didn't seem that interested though. Derek said,

'It must have been some kid in First Year. Only some kid would think of stickers.' – 'Yeah,' I said enthusiastically, 'so dumb!' and at that moment I agreed completely with him. And then I remembered: but it was me – *us*. We're dumb!

Damn! This means if this gets out, it will be seriously embarrassing. What we did is dumb, not cool.

At dinner I got back to questioning my main source, Justine. Apparently everyone in her year was questioned! Because Jayne says she never was racist and Gita says she was so racist, so the teachers are asking if anyone can say what happened. Jayne's friends are backing her up. Gita doesn't have as many people to back her up, which could be because a) she's not as popular as Jayne, or b) because Jayne never actually said anything. She also can't say what exact racist word Jayne used, she just says that her attitude was racist.

'What a mess!' said Mum. 'They'll never sort it out. It comes down to one girl's word against another. Who would you believe?'

'Neither!' said Justine, 'Well, OK, the way they're behaving? I don't think Jayne would have dared say anything racist. Everyone knows that could get you expelled. And anyway I don't think Jayne is actually racist. I think Gita made it up because she knew it was the best way to get Jayne back. And it is! But both parents are *furious*. Jayne's parents are saying it's libel and Gita's parents are saying it's racism!'

'Mr Lucas must be very nervous. Parents have gone to court for less,' said Dad, 'no wonder he called the assembly. He needs to look like he's taking this seriously.'

The racist incident seems to be good for us as a family. At least it is making Justine more talkative and that seems to be making my parents happier but my stomach was a tight, hard ball. I couldn't finish my dinner. I was picking at it bad as Justine. What had we started? Why didn't we ask Gita for PROOF? What were we thinking of? I blame Anna. She's supposed to know about proof and evidence and witnesses. Her oldest brother John is studying law, and she always says she's going to study law too. I've never said I'm going to study law. (I have *no* idea what I'm going to study – not ad campaigns anyway! I am never going to design another poster in my life!).

Later

It has occurred to me that it would be suspicious if I did not mention all this on our blog, so here's what I've posted up:

28th October

The worm has turned! Last week I was reporting on racism in school, but now it seems the racist may not be a racist. Her accuser may be crying wolf. There was certainly a lot of smoke, but no one can tell yet whether there's fire. Even if she, Y, is guilty, she was

condemned without a fair trial. Whoever stickered her was playing prosecutor, judge and
jury.

We say: Innocent until proven guilty!

SOMEONE has a lot to learn.

I am quite proud of this entry. It is cryptic and intriguing, and actually it states my (new) thoughts on the subject. I mean – SOMEONE (a.k.a. me and Anna!) has a LOT to learn. Hope we've learnt it.

THURSDAY OCTOBER 29TH

Oh, great – now me and Anna are fighting.

We haven't learnt anything!

This is the worst week of my life.

Leaving school this afternoon, I just mentioned to her, 'Derek thinks sticking stickers was dumb.'

She said sarcastically, 'I must remember to consult him on cool.'

I said, 'Well, maybe it was babyish.'

Then she lost her temper. I should have seen the signs, I mean her lip was out. She said, 'Trust you to take on someone else's view. You've got no confidence in what you do. You always need to *check* your actions with someone else. And of *course* you would choose a cardboard cut-out definition of cool like Derek to check it with. If you must be such a sheep, try choosing someone

with a bit more cop-on to defer to.'

I said, 'Yeah, well at least I don't always think I'm right. You think you're so great you don't need to ask anyone anything. You think you're above everyone else and whatever you do is perfect. Well some of your ideas are dumb, and you'd be better off checking them.'

She said, '*You* thought of the stickers!'

I said, '*Me*? You did?'

She said, 'You're pathetic,' and stomped off.

I have checked back in this diary to the day we thought of the stickers (October 20th). But all I wrote was, 'Here's what we're gonna do to Jayne …'

How useless is that! What is the point of writing a diary if you leave all the crucial details out? But anyway I *know* she thought of the stickers. Obviously she did! In any case I am fed up with her and her bad moods and her always thinking everyone's an idiot, and just dismissing people. Well now she has dismissed me. Soon she will have no friends at all.

FRIDAY OCTOBER 30TH

Ignored Anna all day in school today. And she ignored me. I wonder if everyone noticed and if they thought it was suspicious? A very intelligent person watching us all week might deduce that we are responsible for the stickers because our behaviour has changed completely this week, but probably no-one is a) very

intelligent, or b) watching us closely. The only people who watch you closely are people who fancy you.

It was weird and not-nice not having Anna to hang round with. Instead at lunch and break I hung round with the rest of the class and I noticed, which I haven't noticed before, that quite a few of them don't have people to hang round with, well they don't have Real Friends, they just have Default Friends. A Real Friend is your best friend or at least someone you really like and *want* to hang round with. A Default Friend is the opposite – it's just someone you are hanging round with for want of someone else. Definition of Default: 'an option that is selected automatically unless an alternative is specified', like on the computer it says: 'your default browser is …' and McMahon says: 'an army's default position …' So there are all these people in the class with only Default Friends, which is sad for them. My main Default Friend today was Heeun – the new girl I told you about from Korea. I guess she is still too new to have made a Real Friend, and like I said, Caroline Hunter abandoned her when it seemed the boys weren't fancying her. But she is actually nice. I talked to her for ten minutes at break and she is quite cool. I think she is quite lonely.

While I was leaving school I saw Anna talking to Gita! I am serious. They left the school gates talking together. That's playing with fire! Someone will notice. I should warn Anna. But I can't.

At dinner I checked in with Justine about what was going on in her class. This week I've talked to her more than I have all year! She said the teachers got Jayne to apologise for bullying, and Gita to admit she might have been paranoid or too quick to point the finger. So Jayne has been cleared of racism, but found guilty of bullying, and Gita has been cleared of libel, but found guilty of stirring things up and told that she should have informed a teacher of any bullying or racism instead of spreading rumours. Both are a little bit wrong and a little bit right. This is a typical teacher way to settle a dispute. Their parents are semi-satisfied. But the hunt for the racist stickers is still on!

SATURDAY, OCTOBER 31ST

It is Hallowe'en today, but I did nothing. Well, in the evening I walked round outside listening to the bangers pop and later on I leaned out the attic window to see fireworks. They were being let off in the distance. Orange and green and red lights exploding. I felt extremely lonely. It is no fun looking at exploding joy by yourself.

I think Mum knows something is up. I caught her looking at me funny. I guess because it's Hallowe'en, she expected me to ask to go round to Anna's.

There was no children's party scheduled, which is odd – you'd think someone would have a Hallowe'en party – but it's also lucky. I don't know what we would have done if there was. I

don't know what we'll do for future children's parties. I suppose Anna might get another partner. The Party People is hers, I concede. Just like the blog is mine.

And the Instruments of Karma is ... whose?

Whoever wants it!

I looked at the blog and I wasn't sure what to do. I felt sad seeing Bomb and Demise up there. Now our friendship is demised. Does this mean the blog is over? Over before it's begun? Or do I announce the demise and keep going solo?

Maybe me and Anna can just make up?

That would be best.

But she needs to apologise. Because she started it.

SUNDAY, NOVEMBER 1ST

Went out for a long walk. Had to get out of the house. It is just so boring there. Justine was moping around as usual.

Walked up to the shopping centre. Only half the shops were open cause it's Sunday. I spent a long time in the DVD library. It is impossible to know which film to rent. There is too much choice. It gets confusing. In the end I took out an old film called *Cruel Intentions*. The back says it is 'a game of seduction and betrayal in a New York High School'. I know all about betrayal anyway! And I need to know about seduction for David Leydon. (But perhaps I am just *naturally* seductive? Because *if* I did seduce Declan, it was without trying!)

Later

Kathryn Merteuil (I just checked this spelling at the back of the DVD, I don't know why she has a French name when she is American. It is pronounced 'Myrrh-toy', like what the wise kings brought baby Jesus) – anyway she would make an excellent Instrument of Karma. We should recruit her! She is extremely devious and cunning and good at manipulating people to get her own way. Although at the end she is found out. Everyone turns against her. I felt extremely uncomfortable watching the end because a) Anna has already turned against me so I know a *bit* how Kathryn felt, and b) if it's discovered we're the racist stickers, the whole school will turn against us, and then I'll know *exactly* how Kathryn felt!

And Kathryn was found out because of her diary! That is a little too close to the bone! I am going to hide this diary a lot better because it Tells All. If Justine found it, she might snitch! Or my mother … well I think it is fair to say my mother would not read my diary. It is lucky Anna has given up keeping a diary because – for sure – Renata would read it, and then she'd tease so badly our lives wouldn't be worth living …

I did not learn too much about seduction. I think seduction in New York High Schools is a lot different to seduction in Dublin secondary schools! Will text to ask Anna what she makes of the different seduction techniques.

Oh…! That last sentence is extremely sad, I think. It is an Elegy to a Demised Friendship.

MONDAY NOVEMBER 2ND

School without Anna is an entirely different place. It is like going to the beach on a cold day. You have to get in the water because that's why you're there. You're not there to sunbathe or relax because there's no sun. You're there to swim. So you get into your togs and shiver and grit your teeth and wade in. And you scream because it's so cold, and you don't stay in long, and then you run out and your teeth chatter for hours.

But it is better to force yourself to speak to people just like it is better to force yourself into the sea. So I spoke to Heeun again. She smiled like she was my friend when I went up to her. She even made a good joke. But she is shy.

Oh, and Declan came up to me. He is the only person who seems to notice that me and Anna are fighting.

He said, 'Where's your other half?'

I was a bit confused, then I got it, and I said, quite defensively, 'She had to finish something …' It is embarrassing to admit we're fighting, I don't know why.

He said, 'Oh, thought you'd had a fight. Not used to seeing one without the other.'

I said, 'Ha, Ha.' There was a kind of an awkward silence.

Then he said, 'So I'm following your blog. Nefarious goings

on in the lower school!' I looked at him suspiciously. That sounded like something Renata would say. I mean what the hell is 'nefarious'? I can't believe that even Declan, who is a computer genius, is getting infected by the way Renata speaks!

I don't know what 'nefarious' means, but I knew what he was getting at. Obviously. He sounded a bit patronising though.

But I was curious so I said, 'Isn't anybody talking about the racist stickers in your class?'

'I'm afraid not. Afraid it hasn't penetrated.'

This is basically a Good Thing. It's definitely good that the whole school isn't talking about who stickered Jayne. But it made me feel embarrassed about making such a deal of it on the blog.

I just looked up 'nefarious' in the dictionary. It means 'atrociously sinful or villainous'. That is a little more extreme than I thought! I thought it meant 'dodgy' or 'unsettling'. I did not realise that me and Anna were atrociously sinful. It's hardly surprising we're not speaking.

TUESDAY NOVEMBER 3RD

Back friends with Anna!

YES!

Oh, and we might get expelled …

What happened was after English (second class) as we were leaving O'Toole said, 'You two, stay!'

He was pointing at me so I stood still and looked around. The other person staying still was Anna! We half glanced at each other. When everyone else had filed out O'Toole closed the door, then he walked behind his desk and drummed his fingers on it, *then* he walked in front of his desk and leaned on it. He gazed out the window, then he looked at us and said, 'Would you say the person who hid Pierce's homework also stuck the stickers on Jayne O'Keeffe?'

Silence! We gaped at him. This was not what I was expecting at all. Then we both spoke at the same time.

Anna said, 'Hid Pierce's homework?'

I said, 'Don't see the connection.'

O'Toole raised his eyebrows at us and looked from one to the other. We'd said completely different things and Anna was implying she didn't know anything about Pierce's homework, while I was implying I did. It was impossible that one of us could know and not the other seeing as we discussed everything, and seeing as he knew we discussed everything. So he paused in a very *deliberate* way, and said to Anna, 'Yes, somebody took Pierce's homework to get him into trouble ...' Then (super ironically), 'Denise will tell you about it.' (We've been studying irony in class. It is quite a difficult concept and I can never remember the definition, but for sure I recognised it now: irony is when you let the other person know that you know they know what you're getting at (whew!).)

Then he said to me, 'The connection is that whoever hid Pierce's homework was trying to punish him for being a bully, and whoever stickered Jayne O'Keeffe was trying to punish her for being a racist. The connection is … street justice.'

There was a silence. It was awful not knowing which way Anna was gonna play this. I couldn't believe how dumb we were not to have prepared for getting questioned. *Criminally dumb*, Renata would say, meaning criminals are dumb otherwise they wouldn't get caught and you wouldn't be labelling them criminals.

Anna said, 'Yeah, I see the connection,' in a very cheerful voice. She didn't sound remotely guilty. I was impressed. She was smiling quite cheekily at O'Toole so I copied her smile, and somehow I understood as if by telepathy from her to me that I shouldn't say anything. Let O'Toole do the talking.

He said, 'Good! So, you'd agree probably the same … *people* did both.' He emphasised *people*.

I said, 'Yeah, I guess, it could have been the same *person*.' I turned full to Anna and looked at her questioningly. She nodded happily at me. We looked back at him.

Then Anna said, 'Though, not necessarily… I mean they're in different years, Pierce and Jayne. It's unlikely someone would have a vendetta against someone in a different year.' She sounded like she was turning this over in a detached way, like it was a subject for debate.

O'Toole said, 'Yes, that's occurred to me. But still, the similarity is striking… If it were someone with … an *over*-pronounced sense of justice, they might transcend year groups, wouldn't you say?'

I shrugged. 'Maybe.' (My shrug was magnificent!)

'Right. So … if I had to pick who did it, I'd say you two.'

Anna said, *'Us?'*

I said, *'Us?'*

He said, 'Acting from good intentions, but not thinking it through. Yes, that would be you two.' (Also in a detached voice, like he was summarising us for a report). He was looking hard at us.

Anna said, 'We're not *that* dumb.' She sounded thoroughly disgusted, like she couldn't believe how dumb the sticker person was.

I said, 'Yeah, and we're not that *good* either.' I giggled and Anna giggled too! We were back on the same wavelength! A feeling warm as toast came over me, even in the middle of my cold worry about being found out.

O'Toole went on, 'And when I see you're not sitting next to each other in class … Such an abrupt change of behaviour … Guilt causes fights, doesn't it?'

We said nothing. I was pretty impressed he'd noticed!

He walked back behind his desk and picked up some papers, 'You'd better get on to your next class,' he said dismissively.

We turned to go. He said, from behind us, 'When something goes wrong, but when you meant well, it's better just to admit it. You'll find people take into account your intentions ... And pleading guilty always gets you a lighter sentence.'

We paused, Anna said, 'I *know* ... but that doesn't apply to us now.'

I turned the handle. As we were walking out, I said, 'Bye, Mr O'Toole.'

He said, 'And of course Jayne deserves an apology ... Not Pierce perhaps. But Jayne, yes. That was libel, you know.'

Anna said, 'Bye, Mr O'Toole,' and we escaped through the door!

In the corridor, Anna muttered, 'Don't say anything. He might come out ...'

So we walked, not too fast, down the corridor, and turned the corner ... Then we turned to each other and both of us went: 'Aaaagghh!' – we opened our mouths very wide and popped our eyes so we looked like cartoon characters. Then we began to run. I don't know why but I had the impulse – and Anna had too I guess – just to run. Because of being so tense the last few minutes maybe, I dunno, but we legged it down the corridors.

So we're back friends! And it's worth it, even if we do get expelled (which we won't, probably, I just put that in for Dramatic Tension).

Mr O'Toole is right: guilt causes fights. But being accused

cements you back together again.

Still we're in trouble and we don't know what to do. O'Toole is On To Us. Somehow. I thought maybe Gita came clean, but Anna said no – Gita told her that when they brought her in for questioning, she totally denied any connection between herself and the stickers. She said she wasn't in school that day, she didn't know anything about it, someone must have heard her accusing Jayne of racism and taken it into their own hands. She stuck to her story.

'That was nice of her!' I said.

'Nah,' said Anna, 'she just knew if she was found out hiring someone to do her dirty work, she'd get into real trouble.'

Anna thinks O'Toole probably doesn't have actual *proof*. She thinks that someone in the class snitched on us about hiding Pierce's homework, and he put 2 and 2 together, and now he is giving us the chance to do the right thing. I said if he doesn't have actual proof he can't pin it on us, and we could just keep on denying everything, like Gita did.

We have agreed to Sleep On It.

Didn't write in the blog. There is no way of writing about O'Toole's accusation without giving the game away.

WEDNESDAY NOVEMBER 4TH

At break we argued it round and round and we didn't get anywhere. On the one hand if we come clean, we will get off lightly –

O'Toole practically promised that – because our intentions were good. On the other hand everyone will then know it was us and they'll think we're dumb (my point). On the other hand Jayne deserves an apology because she probably wasn't actually racist (Anna's point). On the other hand she's been cleared of the charge, more or less, and she *was* bullying – and bullying a girl who was new to Ireland, which is extra mean, even if the girl in question does wear designer shoes – and if we tell, we might get Gita into trouble (my point). On the other hand, Gita deserves to be in trouble seeing as she exaggerated about Jayne being a racist. On the other hand …

Well, you get the picture! There were more hands showing than in netball practice.

So we've decided to ask Tommy. He is the only person we can trust with this.

Oh – at break I caught sight of Heeun coming towards me with this hopeful smile, and then it kind of fading as she saw Anna … but what could I do? It is just tough for her.

Ha! As *if!*

I did not forget the coldness of the sea and the instability of Default Friends. I waved madly so she came up to us and we all chatted away, very friendly.

Afterwards I explained about Default Friends to Anna. She liked that. She thought it was funny. But she said, 'Trust *you* to arrange a default position.'

I said, 'Well what did you do?'

She said in a really superior voice, 'I knew we'd be back friends. I wasn't bothered.'

I said, 'That's because you're used to fighting with your brothers and sister and still being back friends'

'And you're not,' she finished, giving me A Look which I knew was a criticism of the way I can't be bothered with Justine.

I didn't like being criticised and I didn't like her being the one who got to be all cool and solitary, while I scrabbled around un-coolly for default friends, but then I remembered, 'Anyway you'd Carl to speak to.'

She said, 'Carl?' like you'd say *worms?*

I said, 'Yeah. Carl. Your boyfriend.'

I caught her eye. We went off into laughter. Very *mean* laughter.

THURSDAY NOVEMBER 5TH

So after school today we went round to Anna's. In the kitchen were Tommy and Renata and suddenly Anna started telling the whole story to them both! I was amazed. Why would she let Renata in on this? Does she want to be laughed at for the rest of the year? But it was too late to stop her. All I could do was interrupt to make sure she told it right. She kept forgetting crucial things. Maybe because she's given up keeping a diary? Writing things down is a good way of sticking them in your mind.

Tommy and Renata didn't comment at all until the end, which was surprising for Renata. She must have copped how important it was.

When we finished off, 'So what do you think we should do? Come clean to O'Toole, or play dumb?'

Tommy looked at Renata, 'Jesus wept,' he said.

They both looked quite dazed … almost shocked, in a way. I was surprised. I didn't think it would be such a deal. Not to those two – I mean they must have done loads of stuff like that. But apparently not. 'Quite the little Cosa Nostra,' said Renata. (That is something to do with the mafia – I just checked. It means 'our way' in Italian, which, by coincidence, is basically what 'Sinn Fein' means in Irish … I wish people would stop going on about the mafia!)

Tommy said to Renata, 'That pronounced sense of justice … who would have thought it would come to this?'

'When a pronounced sense of justice meets distrust of authority,' said Renata grandly, 'and gets mercenary!' She gave her witchy cackle.

'Maybe not *mercenary* exactly,' said Tommy fairly, 'entrepreneurial …'

'Entrepreneurial! That's one name for it… compromising their standards in pursuit of profit. This shows the *intrinsic* corruption of the capitalist system.'

I was getting mad. I didn't necessarily know exactly what they

were on about but they'd ganged up together – suddenly they were like *parents* – and they were passing judgement and debating our morals, and that's not what we asked them.

'If we wanted a moral lecture, we'd have gone to a priest,' I said, 'just tell us whether we should admit to O'Toole.'

They cracked up laughing – all three! (Good!)

Then Renata said, 'Well *obviously* you have to admit to O'Toole! He knows already. He's just giving you a chance to do the right thing, instead of going straight to Lucas with it.'

'Yeah,' said Tommy, 'I mean what do you think he's gonna do? Just drop it?'

They looked at us as if we were fools. I felt a fool. I mean if it was that obvious, we didn't have to ask their advice, we didn't have to expose ourselves to their moralising.

But, 'Maybe he doesn't know,' said Anna, 'maybe he was *bluffing*. He doesn't have proof. He can't accuse us without *proof*.'

'Oh, it's the lawyer now,' said Renata, 'from anarchist to lawyer. You should have been asking for proof from Gita.'

This was too much!

Anna roared, 'Get lost!' and flung herself on Renata, fists waving.

I screamed, 'Yeah, shut up!' It was total bedlam.

Then Tommy pulled Anna off Renata, 'Okay, that's enough, that's enough!' he was saying in a loud, but firm, not hysterical voice.

After we straightened up, Renata said, 'Alright, I'm sorry, okay? I couldn't resist the dig.'

'You never can,' said Anna.

'I know,' said Renata. She sounded almost ashamed! 'But it wasn't just a dig. I'm your older sister, and I don't know if you realise just how wrong—'

'All right, Renata,' interrupted Tommy, 'let's take it she does. Anyway,' he looked at us and managed to look amused *and* sorry for us at the same time. He has the sort of face that can express a lot of emotions at once, 'Anyway, O'Toole will soon tell them what for. And Lucas too.'

So we have to confess to O'Toole. Tomorrow. We're not going to mention Gita, because Tommy and Renata agreed it would be breaking her trust. We're just gonna say that we heard about the racist incident, and took matters into our own hands, like we took matters into our own hands over Pierce's bullying. We're not gonna mention about the money, obviously. That, as Renata says, would be *wallowing* in our guilt.

On the other hand, *not* mentioning the money makes us sound like do-gooders, like vigilantes dispensing justice. Frankly I'd rather be considered greedy, or – what was it Renata said? – mercenary. (I have just looked this up in the dictionary, it says: Soldier of Fortune and also 'motivated solely by desire for monetary gain'. Soldier of Fortune sounds okay, but we were not motivated *solely* by desire for monetary gain. We were motivated

mostly by desire for monetary gain).

I asked Anna, 'What did you tell Renata for? Now she'll jeer for a year. And what happens if she tells your parents?' Anna looked at me in amazement/contempt, 'She's not gonna tell my *parents*. You don't tell on your brothers and sisters!'

This was obviously a Family Code. I wouldn't know – Justine and me are/were always telling on each other, but then we don't have anywhere else to go. In Anna's family you form factions, and leave the parents out.

FRIDAY NOVEMBER 6TH

Oh God! Sorry, but I am now so bored with the whole thing I could scream!

I know we made a mistake. We've already suffered for it! Five days thinking I'd lost my best friend! Twenty-four hours in a day. 24 x 5 = 120 hours of misery! Which I bet is more than Jayne O'Keeffe suffered.

So we got the full lecture from O'Toole. He must have forgotten that we'd already got the lecture from Lucas at assembly, and he doesn't know we also got it from Tommy and Renata. So yes, we *know*, we're:

a) perhaps well-meaning, but thoroughly misguided;

b) interfering, getting involved in other people's quarrels;

c) egocentric, wanting to take matters into our own hands;

d) secretive, doing nasty things anonymously;

e) bullies, making people's lives miserable;

f) anarchists, not trusting in authority to mete out justice;

g) naïve and foolish, taking other people's words at face value;

h) sloppy, not checking our facts.

Oh, and we're:

i) lucky, because if we hadn't been found out, we would have been set on a murky path that would ended with us as mafia crime lords, like The General or The Penguin (doesn't sound too bad! What a blog I could write then!)

And (faint praise!), we're also:

j) intelligent and contrite, because we came forward.

So we have to take our well-meaning, misguided, egocentric, secretive, bullying, anarchistic, naïve, foolish, sloppy, lucky, intelligent and contrite selves off to see Lucas on Monday …

I got the distinct feeling that O'Toole is well pleased to be reporting how he's solved the Mystery of the Racist Stickers to Lucas. He could not keep a certain satisfaction about how well he's handled this off his (otherwise concerned/grave/sympathetic) face.

SATURDAY NOVEMBER 7TH

Oh, there are more letters in our catalogue. We forgot what Tommy and Renata said about us. So we're also:

k) mercenary, counting our pennies;

l) ruthless capitalists, gradually compromising our standards in pursuit of profit.

Anna says she has hopes we'll make it to z) yet. Our parents will come up trumps! Our parents are going to be informed. Obviously.

SUNDAY NOVEMBER 8TH

It has occurred to me:

a) Tommy and Renata encouraged – made! – us confess because they decided to act like responsible elders, and thought this was the *right* thing to do. They were not acting like our equals. I think this is part of Anna's Family Code. You don't tell the parents, but sometimes you act like the parents. Probably Anna will be giving moralistic / Do the Right Thing advice to Charlie when he's older. But what a pain – maybe we could have got away with not telling!

b) Anna told Renata because she wanted to impress her, because somewhere she (Anna) thought what we did was cool. And even though sometimes she *hates* Renata, she is totally dependent on her good opinion. Maybe that's what it's like having an older brother or sister. Maybe Justine is totally dependent on my good opinion (ha!)

None of this matters of course. Or makes any difference. I am just noting it down for future reference. So when I read over this in twenty years' time I will remember everything.

MONDAY NOVEMBER 9TH

So today we got the lecture from a) to j) all over again from Lucas. He did not manage to add any new letters, which, I said to Anna, seemed a bit lax of him – I thought he'd bring it to m) at least! Anna said, yeah, but it's been pretty well covered already! Well maybe our parents will add some more letters …

We also have to do five hours community service. This is just the kind of very hip/right-on punishment Lucas would come up with.

We also have to write an apology to Jayne O'Keeffe.

But we are not going to be named and shamed in front of the whole school. Apparently this isn't necessary, since we confessed.

Big deal! Like it won't get out anyway. Jayne O'Keeffe will tell everyone.

Fed up and gloomy. This is the sort of situation which could set me and Anna fighting, but luckily we've fought already so we're united in truculence instead (this is Renata's phrase for us – I am thinking of forming a new club to overtake the now-I-suppose-defunct Instruments of Karma: United in Truculence. As United in Truculence we would just go round looking fed-up and stubborn and refusing to get involved in things. It would be quite easy and undemanding).

Oh – and we told Heeun. It will be all over the school – I bet! – next week, and I didn't want her just finding out in the

playground. She is starting to become our friend. When we told her, she went 'Oh-my-God!' and then she began to laugh. In fact she was helpless with laughter. 'That was you two?' She could hardly stand up. She seems to be an enthusiastic person. I do not think she would be very good at being truculent.

TUESDAY NOVEMBER 10TH

Here is our letter to Jayne O'Keeffe:

> *Dear Jayne,*
>
> *We are the racist stickers and we are sorry. We thought you'd been racist and that we were doing the right thing, but now it seems maybe we blackened your name for no good reason. This was misguided of us and the consequences could have been disastrous for you. So now we (the culprits) are coming forward and we're getting seriously punished for it. We hope that you will consider us well served and that you will accept our apology,*
>
> *Yours,*
>
> *Denise Nelson, Anna Power*

I guess we'll have to check this apology with someone, probably Lucas. But we think it's fine. It is sincerely meant but dignified and not too grovelling or chest-beating. I mean we're being properly punished. I don't see why we should have to grovel too.

Like Anna says, it is demeaning to have to write such a letter to a *First* Year. The shame could kill us. If we were those Japanese prisoners of war that McMahon told us about we would commit suicide rather than face the shame.

WEDNESDAY NOVEMBER 11TH

We were right that our parents would add more letters to the catalogue. Here's what mine added:

m) deluded, living in a fantasy world, thinking I'm the star of some third-rate soap opera;

n) altogether-too-pleased-with-myself – (this one could come under b) egocentric, but it seems to have a meaning beyond that even, so I'm giving it a letter of its own. Apparently all I ever consider is my own enjoyment. I ride rough-shod over anyone and everyone in the pursuit of my own pleasure. Golly!)

And, of course,

o) showing off. I am surprised it took till o) for someone to mention showing-off, because that is normally the first thing hurled at you. I was about to argue – how could we be showing off when it was anonymous – but I didn't because a) we – me and Anna – had agreed our strategy with our parents: hang our heads and act meek, this is the quickest way for the storm to pass; and b) I suddenly remembered the blog, I guess I was kind of anonymously showing off in the blog…

To add to the five hours community service, here is my home

punishment: Grounded for a week, and No Telly.

Texted Anna:

we are also deluded show odds...

I wonder how she is getting on? They can't deny her telly because she's permanently denied telly. So her punishment is probably more elaborate (and worse) than mine.

Later

We have reached r)! I think if we did a vox pop – you know asking random people in the street what they think – we would reach z). Easy.

According to Anna's parents, we are:

p) wasteful – expending our energy on something that pays no profit. That was from her Dad (of course) and that's the one that really hurt Anna. Of course she was dying to explain that it was anything but wasteful, but she didn't (thank God!).

q) irresponsible, throwing the cat among the pigeons in a class of people younger and therefore more vulnerable than ourselves;

r) suffering *égoisme à deux*. This is a French sigh-chiatrist's way of saying we're too wrapped up in each other. It means: 'two people neurotically 'in love' who feel no love for anybody else'. Whoa!! Calm down! We do so love other people! Anna loves Charlie and Tommy and I love … hmm? … David Leydon … J.P… (not seriously, though!) Well I love my parents – obviously!

Anna said her mum took it really seriously. In fact, as she was talking about *égoisme à deux* she began to wonder out loud if maybe we were spending too much time together and if we should be separated!!!

Huh!! And I thought her mum was my *friend!*

Well if that were my mum saying that I'd have gone nuts, but Anna managed to be (unusually) diplomatic. She just kept quiet and waited for her mum to argue the whole thing around. Apparently she started off saying we should be 'forcibly separated' but then argued that this might be 'counterproductive' and make us 'stubbornly refuse to move on'. She concluded that it was better 'not to force the issue. They'll probably outgrow each other.'

Why, thanks Mrs Power!! I love you too!

Anna's punishment is to give the next takings of a children's party – we have one on Sunday – to a charity. Well, not *a* charity, Amnesty International since they combat racism, bullying, persecution of the weak, the interfering by strong states into the affairs of the weak and all the other things we're guilty of.

There is something – I dunno – *creepy* about this punishment. But Anna doesn't seem to mind too much. Perhaps because of her social conscience. The flip side of her greed to *make* money is her desire to give it *away* (to charity). This is not like me. I don't care about making it so much, and I'm not that motivated to give it away.

THURSDAY NOVEMBER 12TH

Today we had to give Jayne O'Keeffe our letter. O'Toole made us re-write it. He said, 'That is a totally inadequate letter. Your use of the word "blackened" shows inappropriate levity. Your apology is self-regarding. You contributed to a major upset and you need to *grovel. Mea culpa, mea culpa, mea maxima culpa!*' and he thumped his heart theatrically each time he said '*mea culpa*'. Whatever all that meant. Well, what it meant was we had to re-write.

Here is our final attempt (fourth draft). It is more O'Toole than us. It is a forced confession. It was practically beaten out of us:

Dear Jayne,

We are the racist stickers and we are truly sorry. We believed you'd been racist and that we were doing the right thing, but now we understand that we libelled you on insufficient evidence. This was misguided and stupid and unfair of us and the consequences could have been disastrous for you. We understand that we must never ever ever accuse anyone ever without hearing their side of the story. We are glad we learnt this lesson young but are so sorry that it was at your expense. As punishment we are doing community service. We hope that you will consider us well served and

that you will accept this apology, which is sincerely meant,
Yours,
Denise Nelson, Anna Power

So then O'Toole took us to Lucas' office for the All Apologies Session. Jayne was called in.

Lucas said, 'Denise and Anna have something to say.'

We said, 'It was us, sorry,' and handed her the letter.

She looked quite shocked and suddenly I looked at her and she wasn't oozing popularity and bitchiness. She looked awful. She looked like she'd had a worse week than me even. So I said sorry again and this time I meant it.

Afterwards Anna said, 'Well, I do feel bad actually ...'

I said 'Yeah, because she looked ... but she *is* a bully!'

And Anna said, 'Yeah, but we don't know what happened exactly. We'll never know. Probably Jayne and Gita don't even know any more, the story's got so confused. But the thing is ... there are people in this school who are always going to think she's racist and that's because of us making a big deal of it.'

'Maybe she's learnt a valuable lesson,' I said hopefully, 'never put yourself in a position where people can accuse you.'

'Maybe *we've* learnt a valuable lesson.'

'Well, of course *we* have! No telly and no money and public humiliation, probably ...'

FRIDAY NOVEMBER 13TH

Well I was right about the public humiliation. Jayne has told everyone. I can't really blame her. We are trying to keep our dignity but it's not that easy. Most people are treating it as *hilarious*. 'Ooh,' they say when we approach, 'careful! It's the vigilantes!'

Is it better to be a) a laughing stock, or b) have people despise you, or c) scared of you?

a) is better than b) but I think I'd prefer c).

SATURDAY NOVEMBER 14TH

Well the school might think we're a) a laughing stock, but it seems that my own little sister b) despises us!

After breakfast today, she came up and said, 'So it was you and Anna?'

And I said, 'Yeah, okay! We messed up! Don't rub it in!' in a pretty nasty, snappy voice, but it is hard being laughed at and I needed to snap at someone, and what else are little sisters for?

She said, 'You really did mess up. You couldn't do it right and then you got found out.'

I said, 'Enough already! If I wanted a lecture at home, I'd have invited Lucas and O'Toole to dinner.'

She said, 'Yeah, well you've just made it worse.' And she stomped upstairs.

I was pissed off – families should stand up for each other! – but

now it's occurred to me that Justine has added another letter, so we're also:

s) Incompetent messers, not able to do a job properly without being found out.

It's pretty smart of Justine to have worked that out. In fact, now that I think about it, we owe Gita her money back. We didn't carry out our mission properly. Obviously it will kill Anna to do this, but she is very fair-minded. She is (probably) more fair-minded than she is mercenary.

SUNDAY NOVEMBER 15TH

There was actually an issue about my doing the children's party today, because I'm grounded. I was amazed.

I said, 'It's *work*, not fun, how can that be grounded?' Mum said, 'I think you get quite a lot of fun out of it, and grounded means grounded, means not leaving the house.'

So I thought incredibly fast and said, 'Well, yes, but that would mean letting these people down when I made a commitment to them' – she is big into not letting people down and keeping to your commitments – 'and,' I said, 'I'll give half to charity!'

So she agreed, but then she said, 'Charity begins at home,' so I said, 'How do you mean?' wondering did she want me to give half to her and Dad because the recession had taken all our money, which seemed a bit weird and a bit scary, but she said, 'When you were trying to find out what was happening with

Jayne and Gita I noticed you talking more to Justine and trying to engage her, but now … you're just ignoring her again, aren't you? I think a little more charity to your younger sister is in order.' So I said, 'Oh!' quite relieved because we aren't actually poor, it was just the same old parent complaint, so I said, 'OK, sure, of course – I can talk to her!' like it was no big deal. I didn't say that Justine had insulted me and added another letter to the catalogue, because I knew one word would set my mother off and I wanted to get to the party.

It was another really easy party to manage, which was good at the time but means I've nothing to feed the blog with. It's strange that our first party was such a disaster. It's like we passed a test and now it will never be so hard again. Maybe it's because we're more experienced – for instance we'd never arrive now with the cake we baked for Chloe – but it's not just that. Chloe's party had a lot of difficult characters (including her parents!) whereas today there were only seven guests and they were all angelic. It was like they'd been brought up by Barney to love each other, and hadn't yet realised that he's actually a sinister dinosaur who is brainwashing children for some nasty purpose of his own. But the birthday girl's parents were really cool. And we got a tip! The dad gave us an extra €10! He was really nice and actually quite young and actually quite handsome – I said he looked like Colin Farrell, and Anna said, no, Jonathan Rhys Myers. I do not see how he could look like both and anyway, I

said, he had dark hair, not light; 'Try looking beyond the obvious' said Anna in a very superior voice, 'so if I put on a long, black wig, I'd be Angelina Jolie, would I?' Then we both dissolved laughing cause Anna could not look less like Angelina Jolie. One of those indie actresses maybe, but not remotely like Angelina Jolie! Anyway whoever he looked like, the dad was quite handsome and quite rich and quite generous and is not suffering in the recession!

So then we had to work out did Anna have to give all her tip up to Amnesty International, and me half my tip up? I said, no, that definitely wasn't in the contract. She said she knew she wasn't *legally* obliged, but *morally* she felt she was.

I said, 'If you want to know about morals, go ask a priest.'

She laughed. This is becoming my catch-phrase.

Anyway she is giving *all* her tip up and she has a holier-than-thou look (according to me). I'm not giving *any* of my tip and I have a cunning, greedy look (according to her).

MONDAY NOVEMBER 16TH

Actually we *don't* have to give Gita her money back.

This morning Anna said, 'Gita *lied* to us, right? Saying Jayne was a racist?'

I said, 'Yeah! Well, I suppose she might have misunderstood Jayne ...'

'Whatever! Lucas has decided Jayne was falsely accused, so

really *Gita* should be paying *us*!'

'Yeah! Right!' I said again, 'and anyway she's managed to keep out of this and get no blame … if we approach her, we'll compromise her …'

'She'll probably run away screaming …'

So at least we make €10.50 from this!

Trust Anna to find a way out of paying back!

J.P. has rumbled us! At break he came up to us and said, 'Tell me you got paid for that?'

He was looking down at us (he is quite tall) with his small, red eyes (I mean they are not actually red, he isn't a demon, they are pale blue, but red-rimmed). I looked at his arms. His sleeves were rolled up and he'd no coat though it was pretty windy, but he never wears a coat. His arms are the only conventionally handsome thing about him, they are long and tanned and vein-y. It is funny his arms are tanned when his face is white. I got the goosebumps and felt myself turning into a flailing mess. This is the effect he has on me. It is a real tragedy that I can't feel cruel and powerful like I do with Declan.

Then both me and Anna admitted (proudly, defiantly), 'Well, yeah …'

'So who paid you?' His eyes gleamed red. He looks like a member of the rodent family, definitely. Not a rat, but maybe a stoat or a weasel. Luckily we weren't so far gone as to say who paid us (we shouldn't even have admitted we got paid, but no

way was I gonna come across as a do-gooder to J.P. and even Anna wasn't).

We said, 'Can't say!' and then Anna looked at him fiercely and said, 'Hey, you're not to say we got paid, right? We're in enough trouble.'

A kind of electric charge passed between her and him. The fact is that round J.P. there are a lot of charges. He is like an electrical storm. But none from him to me, ever. (Damn! Damn! Damn!) He said, 'Won't say a thing – but imagine getting caught!' And he gave his jeering, good-natured, dangerous laugh.

At the end of lunch break, going back to class, I caught sight of Anna's coat; it had a sticker saying: **Lame-oid**! on it. I peeled it off. She checked my back. Same sticker.

This, as Anna says, is inevitable. But although we are acting very cool/relaxed/nonchalant/unconcerned and although this is nearly doing the trick – people aren't getting a rise out of us so they're not making as much of the whole thing as they could – still they're making *something* of it, and it's beginning to get us down. Back in Anna's kitchen today, her mum said, 'How are you two doing?' in a nice, kind voice. I just looked at her suspiciously because I know about her secret desire to get rid of me. Anna made a sighing/grunting/fed-up noise.

Her mum said, 'Well the worst is over.'

I said gloomily, 'The whole school knows now.'

Renata said, 'A week is a long time in politics.'

I've decided to come clean on the blog. Why not? Since everyone knows and we've given up the Instruments of Karma anyway, I might as well. So I wrote:

The game is up. The racist stickers (see last week's blog) have been rumbled. And... it is us! Bomb and Demise. Since the whole school now knows you might as well know.

We put our hands up: we made a mistake! We've apologised. Here's the letter we wrote to our victim, Y:

[then I inserted our letter to Jayne]

And now this chapter's closed!

(If I inform my readers it's closed, perhaps it will be! (Hmm, what readers? Twenty hits, but no comments ...)

TUESDAY NOVEMBER 17TH

I'm worried about our book and music choices. I think maybe they look a bit try-hard cool, so I texted Anna:

name of a book you think is asap but you still egg

(aka name me a book you think is crap but you still dig)

She texted back:

The Curious Incident of the Dog in the Night-time

I texted:

not asap enough!

(Actually, not asap at all, Anna!)

So then:

The dc vinci code

This will have to do. I will put it up on blog to make her look less try-hard. It is not as out there as *Crime and Punishment*. But how come she's so obsessed with murders?

I am also gonna put Britney in my Music because I think she's asap but I still egg her …

Declan came up to us at break.

He said, 'So Bomb and Demise … you're the racist stickers!'

I forgot he'd be following our blog, of course.

Anna said, 'Enough already,' in a dangerous voice.

He didn't hear the danger. He said, 'Did you plan the whole thing to spice up your blog?'

Anna said scornfully, 'We're not that *stupid*.'

And I said wittily, 'And we're not that *smart*.'

And we both began to giggle. He looked at us in his confused, despairing, way. Then Anna suddenly said in a nice voice, 'But you're right, I mean, if we were really cunning, we *could* have planned it … Do you think it reads like a good story?'

He said eagerly, 'Yeah, well it had that element of surprise, didn't it? And it's something to follow, not just your likes and dislikes.' He looked at me.

I said, 'Yeah, well it's over now. Closed chapter,' in a snappy kind of voice. He went off.

Anna looked at me, 'There's no need ... he's not *insulting* you.'

'I *know*!' I felt really guilty. I was not behaving like that on purpose. There is something about him that makes me want to torture him is all.

WEDNESDAY NOVEMBER 18TH

Actually Declan might be right that this incident has spiced up our blog – I logged on today and found a comment posted up!!

well racist stickers, you HAVE let a bomb off. Or two bombs? Are x and y demised? who rumbled you?

The comment was from curiousinDenver. Amazing!! We have an interested *and* witty reader a million miles away!!

I uploaded:

Our intentions were good. We thought we were clearing the school of racism! We thought the situation needed a bomb. But we were mistaken. The racist wasn't so racist and our informer wasn't informing right... So now we know (cause we've been told), we're: well-meaning but misguided, interfering, egocentric, secretive, bullying, anarchistic, naive, foolish, sloppy, lucky, intelligent, contrite,

mercenary, ruthless, deluded, wasteful, nar-
cissistic messers!!

This is a lot to take in!

We're grounded and we're doing community
service and we're giving money to charity and
we're putting up with the whole school
jeering.

Our bombs did not cause demises! X and Y are
just fine.

But maybe *we'll* be demised …!

And maybe this chapter is not closed after all!

THURSDAY NOVEMBER 19ᵀᴴ

There is actually a discussion about us on the blog! Three people
are in on it. This is just incredible!

And they seem to be on our side!

From Heimlich manoeuvre:

well at least you have taken some action
against perceived injustice!

From curiousinDenver:

yeah, you guys acted a bit hastily, but it's
cool you got indignant and didn't just sit on
your asses about it!

From Pippa:

I don't think this is the demise of you!
(hope not!!!)

Anna just called and said (in a German accent), 'Vell, at least vee hof taken zum ack-tchung against perceived injustice, yah!'

I said (in an American accent), 'Yeah, man, we din jus sit around on our asses, man.'

We are big in Denver and Germany!

FRIDAY NOVEMBER 20TH

A new and pertinent question from xenawarrior cleaner:

do you two get paid for hiding home-work/sticker-ing, or do you just have a super-hero complex???

Not sure how to answer this.

Now Anna's getting into the blog. She has been leaving it all to me but the thought of our global supporters is getting her going. She did a quite funny thing. She took photos of the stickers and uploaded them:

1. A photo of the sticker saying **RACIST!** (black on yellow) and an arrow:

what we stuck on Y's back!

2. Then: photo of the sticker saying *Lame-Oid!* and an arrow:

what was stuck on our backs!

Oh – good news! Heeun is having a party next Saturday. And I won't be grounded by then so I can go. And David Leydon

might be there! (He is invited but of course he might not come. He might think it sounds too babyish. He might be going to a Death Metal club or be spending the night in a graveyard).

SATURDAY NOVEMBER 21ST

I am off to do my community service. I have to do two and a half hours today and two and a half tomorrow. The school arranged it. I think they spoke to a) Fr Bailey (our religion teacher) and b) the youth club, and c) our parents. So I am helping in a soup kitchen in town and Anna is helping asylum-seeker families learn English.

I can't believe we're not in the same place! This is way hard! I have the feeling our parents insisted on this. Anna's mum rang my mum the other day and I tried to eavesdrop but she took the phone into her bedroom so I couldn't but I bet they agreed we were seeing too much of each other.

We are not going to crumble in the face of their pathetic attempts to separate us!

Later

It is very hard work making soup for two hundred people. I had just one job which was chopping carrots. The carrots are donated by kind shops. It is a pity they aren't donated by supermarkets, where they're ready-chopped! But now I am wondering whose job it is to ready-chop all the carrots in the bags in

supermarkets. I now feel very sorry for these people. But maybe supermarkets have machines to do it? It would be nice if they donated these machines to the soup kitchens!

But except for my arm dropping off – and the fact that I will never again be able to eat a carrot – it was fine, actually quite fun. The other volunteers were nice. They were a lot older than me. They asked me what I was doing there. Obviously it is not usual for 2nd Years to help in soup kitchens and they thought I was a very religious person. I considered playing up to this and saying in a very pious voice that I was there to help my fellow man who was less fortunate than myself but I didn't because a) it would have sounded nauseating and b) it is not very religious to lie about being religious. So I told the truth, the whole truth, and nothing but the truth. It was a good story to amuse us while we chopped and peeled and grated. They thought it was hilarious, except one of them said in a sniffy voice that she didn't see that this – working in the soup kitchen – was a *punishment* and I real-ised that it wasn't very tactful of me to put it like that, but then Agnes – she's the lady who organises things and tells us what to do – rolled her eyes at me, so that was okay.

But then this guy came in and he was quite mad, as in mad insane, not mad angry. He had a big box of potatoes which he dumped triumphantly on the table. He had an enormous amount of energy – even before he spoke, you knew he'd shout, and shout he did.

'How are you today?' he shouted at Agnes, and then before she had a chance to answer, he shouted, 'All new potatoes!'

He was just like Mr Noisy. I looked at his feet to see if he was wearing big clumpy shoes, but in fact he was just wearing runners with quiet, rubber soles. Maybe someone insisted he wore them to tone him down? Then he went to the sink and began washing the potatoes with maximum noise – splosh! splash! scrub! – and he broke into a cheerful song all about sheeps, or sheets, or sheaves. He did not have such a brilliant voice.

His presence was a disturbance in the force. No place for our nice, quiet chat now. But he didn't stay long. He finished those potatoes with maximum speed – I have to admit, his scrubbing technique was much more impressive than mine – and then he was off, whistling loudly. Nobody said anything bad about him when he was gone because a) this was a soup kitchen where people don't say bad things about people, and b) he is obviously a helpful person – but everybody relaxed as soon as he left the room, I did notice that.

He was back again to serve the soup though. They let me serve the soup too, and this was a nice change from chopping carrots. Most of the people getting soup were men. They were nice to us. They said 'Thanks love'. Some of them looked like homeless people you see on the street, but some of them looked completely normal. Agnes says since the recession, there are many more people coming in who used to do normal jobs and it is not

their fault their jobs disappeared. It's a bit like if no one had any money they wouldn't be able to hire Anna and me to do their children's parties, which would mean we wouldn't have a job and it wouldn't be our fault. (But when our job as the Instruments of Karm ended, it *was* our fault).

Afterwards we cleared up and stacked this enormous dishwasher (it is lucky someone donated an enormous dishwasher, the washing-up would have taken forever!) Then Agnes made some tea. I do not normally like tea, but this tea was delicious because I was so tired after all the work.

I discovered that I actually did three and a half hours, but I am not counting. Well I am *counting*, but I am not *holding* to account.

Wonder how Anna got on?

SUNDAY NOVEMBER 22ND

Came back very tired this afternoon, very tired. I love Agnes, but it is very tiring chopping, and scrubbing, and serving, and clearing, and stacking.

When I came in the door, Dad said, 'Carrots?'

I said tragically, 'Onions!' and raised my reddened eyes to his.

It was a good moment between us.

When we sat down to table, Mum said brightly, 'Carrot soup for starters!'

I said, 'Waa-ugh!'

They all started laughing, even Justine. She sometimes has a good sense of humour in a quiet way. She is quiet like Dad and I am chatty like Mum. It wasn't carrot soup, obviously. It was fish pie, which I devoured because I was starving. Justine said she didn't really like fish pie, but she ate some of the potato top.

Mum said, 'But darling, you hardly like anything, it seems.'

I was about to give Justine a lecture on the homeless and how grateful they'd be to get something that wasn't carrot soup, but I didn't. I was feeling tired and suddenly I thought Agnes wouldn't like me saying that.

After dinner I decided to write up my soup kitchen experiences on the blog. I think our readers must be done debating our vigilante-ism. They need some new entries. But Anna had got there before me. This is what she wrote:

```
As punishment for stickering Y, we have been
sent on community service. We have been sent to
serve different communities because they [our
parents and teachers] are afraid that the com-
bination of bomb and demise is too explosive.
So I (Bomb) went off to give English conversa-
tion classes to asylum-seekers and she
(Demise) went to a soup kitchen.
I will tell you something: the situation of
asylum seekers is a disgrace! My blood is boil-
ing!! I think that I am going to make some more
```

racist stickers and stick them on the backs of all of the ministers and on the Taoiseach [our prime minister].

No, seriously, the only thing I can do at the moment is teach asylum seekers better English so they can express themselves, but when I grow up I am gonna be a lawyer and then I will argue racism upfront in court instead of having to make behind the back accusations (well, stuck on the back accusations!)

Wow! I do not even need to speak to Anna anymore. I can follow her life on the blog.

MONDAY NOVEMBER 23RD

Well, Anna must have spent all weekend talking to her family about asylum-seekers because she bombarded me with a load of information as soon as I got into school. I cannot remember all of it, but apparently their situation is a disgrace (which I already knew from the blog). I wished I had something about homeless people to give her but unfortunately I did not spend all weekend getting information on them. So it seemed from our conversation that asylum-seekers were much worse off than homeless people. This doesn't seem fair. I feel I am letting my homeless people down by not sticking up for them as being the worst off.

Anna says she is going back next weekend to continue her

classes. That figures. But actually, although I do not have such a strong social conscience, I know what she means and I might even go back myself. I would like to see Agnes. Probably she is a saint. Anyone who puts up with Mr Noisy must be a saint.

TUESDAY NOVEMBER 24TH

Dissent on the blog!

Pippa has posted up:

you girls need to get out more! targeting racists and helping asylum seekers ... it's cool but stop carrying the cares of the world on your shoulders. go play in the traffic ...

From Xenawarrior cleaner:

yeah, paint your nails electric blue, back-comb your hair ...

But from curiousinDenver:

no! your idealism is inspiring!

From Glasshouses:

you don't know what you are talking about about Asylum Seekers. These people should not be let in!

I feel dizzy. I think I agree with Pippa and Xena.

Did not write anything back.

It's lucky Heeun is having a party this Saturday. We can get out and backcomb our hair and drop the cares of the world from

our shoulders, and our readers will realise we have a life and are not just do-gooders.

WEDNESDAY NOVEMBER 25TH

Oh God! Our blog is a writhing mass. It has spawned! I mean the comments are giving birth to *more* comments and *those* comments to more comments … New add-ons are Hirohito and ZeeZee and Eloise at the Holiday Inn. They are all having a good old debate about us! O'Toole would be very impressed: everyone is marshalling their arguments and all sides are covered.

Hirohito:

I wish you would come to my school because nobody is making a stand here!

ZeeZee:

Maybe you mean well, Bomb and Demise, but I am afraid you are patronising little colonialists.

Eloise at the Holiday Inn:

Well what can you expect from someone who likes Britney?

Miaaow, Eloise!

I'm afraid we have created a monster. I am terrified to write anything. They'll all dive on it and they'll be a feeding frenzy and my poor little comment will end up covered in blood and ripped apart … But Anna has got stuck in.

She has posted up:

It is better to risk looking like an idiot than to do nothing p.s. it's called irony Eloise

That is quite good, especially the p.s., but I think I am going to warn Anna not to get involved. It is brave, but reckless. They might come and get us! Probably they are all excellent hackers, and they know where we live …

THURSDAY NOVEMBER 26TH

Had nervous dream. I do not remember much about it now but it was very frenzied and all the way through a voice was intoning gravely: 'throw the baby out with the bathwater'. That is what I woke up saying: 'throw the baby out with the bathwater.'

This does not make any kind of sense.

But someone was definitely pursuing me in the dream. And that does make sense.

I think I am terrified of our blog. Did not log on today.

FRIDAY NOVEMBER 27TH

I am gonna help Heeun prepare her party tomorrow. This means I cannot go to the soup kitchen. There is not time to help two people, and it's important to help your friends (I think). Anna is going to the asylum-seekers (of course).

Actually I am gonna go to the soup kitchen on Sunday. Heeun wants to come too. Turns out she is actually big into going to mass and helping people. We are going to go together because – this is the good bit – I am staying over at Heeun's after the party! I am really surprised that I'm allowed to because normally there is never any staying over at houses after parties. (I dunno what parents think is gonna happen to us if we don't return to our OWN beds after parties, but they certainly think the WORST). I have a feeling my being allowed stay over is part of the plot to separate me from Anna and get me new friends. What they don't know is that Anna is staying over too! (Ha!)

Snuck a look at the blog. I cannot resist it though it is giving me nightmares … Anna's last comment has started a whole new trend. It seems to be a Famous Quotations Trend.

curiousinDenver wrote;

Yes, exactly Bomb! All it takes for evil to triumph is for good men to do nothing.

Hirohito:

All your troubles start when you leave your room… so stay home Bomb and Demise!

Heimlich manoeuvre:

You can fool some people some of the time but you can't fool all the people all of the time.

I don't see what the last quote has to do with anything but I guess it's nice that our blog is attracting such well-educated readers.

I could not resist. I wrote:

Pippa and Xena, we are taking your advice (and sorry Hirohito we are disregarding yours!) – tomorrow we are leaving our rooms and going to a party. We will paint our nails electric blue and drop the cares of the world from our shoulders (who cares if they SMASH??!!)

It is rash of me to encourage them by responding – especially after I warned Anna off – but they really want a response and I find it very difficult not to give people what they want.

SATURDAY NOVEMBER 28TH

Do not have a lot of time to write this. Just back from helping Heeun. Must have dinner, then shower, then dress, then go back to Heeun's and have fun (that is an order!)

Heeun's house is large and has a lot of beautiful things – vases and carpets and statues and lamps – and it is tidy as a hotel. Her dad is the ambassador, that's why. She never mentioned this, which shows that she must be a nice person (I think). There was no sign of her parents, Mr and Mrs Ambassador. Perhaps they at a reception? There were a lot of servants though! They are all Korean and they did not speak to us. This made me pretty uncomfortable. At Anna's house they have a cleaning lady, Mrs

O'Reilly, but she speaks all the time. She can speak and wash up and iron and feed Charlie all at once, so you do not feel embarrassed. In my house we do not have servants or a cleaning lady but then we are not a) ambassadors nor b) have lots of children.

Anyway because of all the servants, I don't think Heeun needed me to help her. Probably the servants could have put black paper around the lampshades and put out crisps and peanuts into bowls and plugged in disco lights and moved the stereo into the basement – that is where the party will be. But it was nice for Heeun to have me there, I can see that, she is quite nervous about how it is going to go.

So am I!

I am wearing this kind of long t-shirt, which could be a mini-dress but I am wearing it over leggings which makes it a t-shirt (I think), and my Doc Martens and loads of bracelets, and two necklaces. I will scrunch up my hair into a wild style. This is all quite daring for me. Normally I am just in jeans and t-shirt.

SUNDAY NOVEMBER 29TH

Today Mr Noisy shouted at me, 'And how are you today?'

I said, 'Good … what about you.'

'Me. I'm great, of course,' he shouted, 'The Boss is here!'

'The Boss?' I said, looking round.

'The Boss!' he shouted, 'Jesus Christ. The Boss is here!'

Agnes rolled her eyes. Heeun looked amazed.

Now every time I think of Jesus I see him in a suit behind a huge desk with an American accent. The Boss.

I hope that Mr Noisy has not stuck this image of Jesus in my mind for ever. I don't think it can be right.

It is very impressive Heeun and I managed to go to the soup kitchen and Anna to the asylum-seekers considering how incredibly late we got to bed and how incredibly tired we were. There was a moment when all three of us might have just said 'forget about it' and stayed on sleeping.

But then Anna said – from her mattress – 'the thick thug throttled the thrush by the throat' like she'd been saying it all night in her dreams, and I knew she was preparing her lesson for the asylum seekers because she'd explained that the 'th' sound is difficult for foreigners – so I said (from my mattress) 'carrots, carrots, carrots'.

Then Heeun said (from her bed), 'I will get scrambled eggs and toast for us.'

'And orange juice?' I said, and got up.

I was glad I did. It was even good to see the carrots and Mr Noisy.

Oh the party?

Well, that will have to wait. I am exhausted, and my fingertips and even my eyeballs have turned orange from all the carrots, and the only thing going through my heavy and exhausted mind is: the thick thug throttled the thrush by the throat the thick

thug throttled the thrush by the throat what did the thick thug throttle who throttled the thrush by the throat what was the thrush throttled by what did the thick thug do to the thrush ...

MONDAY NOVEMBER 30TH

Just checked the blog. Pippa has posted up:

So???? What about the party?

And Xenawarriorcleaner:

what no word??? Is it too much to hope you went mental and are still sleeping it off???

It is nice that people are so interested (I guess), but it is kind of alarming too.

So the party. First things first: I looked quite good. My hair looked punky and wild, but not a mess. Even mum and dad said I looked nice. I waited till I got to Heeun's to put on make-up because I'm not allowed wear it. Heeun looked great! She was wearing a white dress with big red flowers on it. It looked like a really very expensive dress. It was daring of Heeun to wear it because it was almost girlie pretty, and it's not cool to look girlie pretty (well, Anna and me don't think so) but she got away with it (the dress didn't actually have frills. It did not go *that* far!) Then Anna arrived. She was wearing jeans and a t-shirt, as usual, and her hair was short and neat, as usual, and she didn't put on any make-up, as usual, so in fact she might have been calling round to watch a DVD, not go to a party. She is a very consistent

person. Me and Heeun found this reassuring. We were nervous enough about our own outfits. At least one of us was as usual.

People began to arrive. Practically the whole class was invited and some of them brought friends. So there were a lot of people. Heeun's basement can take a crowd. You'd never get that amount of people into my house. It was interesting that her parents a) let her invite so many people and b) weren't even there! A lot of adults – servants – were there and one of them, Myung, seems to be Heeun's nanny, or housekeeper, or stand-in-mum or pseudo-mum or whatever you want to call her. So we had supervision, but still! Luckily our parents did not know we were unparented! There was a big stereo system and most people brought music. Actually too many people brought too much music and soon there were the stereo wars. The battle of musical tastes! Caroline Hunter would put on Rihanna or Kanye West and she and her friends would start dancing and then Ben would put on My Chemical Romance or something (I can't pretend I know all the names of the bands he listens to) and he and his friends would start jumping around – pogo-ing or whatever it's called – and Caroline and her friends would howl. It was a real mess and actually – for once! I agreed with Caroline because I like some of Ben's music, sure, but you can't precisely *dance* to it. Well the class – those who were keeping out of the stereo wars – didn't know what to do. They were willing, but confused, they'd start bopping dancing and then they'd start pogo-ing (some of

them) and then they'd just sit down.

So luckily Anna took charge. At least she took Heeun firmly by the arm and said, 'Heeun, you have to sort this out' because it was Heeun's word, of course it was, it was Heeun's party.

So Heeun said, 'For one hour it is Caroline's music, and then you can have your choice, Ben.'

She managed to say it quite firmly, almost as well as Anna. Perhaps that is her ambassador's training. Or perhaps it's that she had Anna beside her, which is like having a bulldog beside you. Anyway it worked. Truce in the stereo wars! The girls began dancing (and some of the boys too, pretending to do taking-the-piss dancing, but actually secretly enjoying it).

Then J.P. arrived and the whole atmosphere changed. Suddenly all the girls were dancing to him (even though they weren't necessarily looking at him, they were definitely dancing *to* him). He took a quick look round the party and saw that it was un-parented.

So then he came sauntering up to me and Anna with his hands scrunched into the pockets of his tight jeans, 'Let's do a whip around and send someone to the off-license.'

Our jaws dropped. 'For *beer*?' I squeaked.

'Well not for Fanta,' he said sarcastically.

He'd gone crazy. I couldn't even begin to say what was wrong with his plan, but a) it wasn't like we were all carrying money – I mean why would we be? We didn't need it at the ambassador's

reception – and b) *who* were we going to send to an off-license? Some people look sixteen, maybe, but nobody looks eighteen, let alone twenty-one, and c) nobody else wanted booze. J.P is just a lot more advanced than the rest of us. So his plan was crazy and probably he knew this and was just trying it on. Anna and I decided to go along with it, cause we knew it wasn't going to happen.

We said, '*right!*' in a 'you-can-count-on-us' way and went round to everyone, saying importantly, 'Do you have any money? Cause J.P.'s gonna go to the off-license?'

So of course everyone turned their pockets inside out for J.P., but it was like I guessed, nobody really had any money on them. It made us all feel important that J.P was asking us, but the truth is we were at a house party that our parents had driven us to and our parents would be picking us up from. J.P. obviously thought he was at another kind of party, an older party, where people fended for themselves and bought beer.

'No go,' I said to Anna. She said, 'Yeah…' then 'we'd better warn Heeun.'

So we went up to her and Anna said, 'J.P. is gonna come up and ask you to get money to send someone to the off-license, so you'd better say no, okay?'

Heeun looked totally panic-stricken – poor her, wouldn't you, saying no to J.P.? – but she said, 'Okay …'

And this was super well-guessed of Anna cause when we told

J.P. That no one had any money, he got his most jeering expression, and said, 'Losers,' but then he said 'but there's money somewhere' and his red eyes gleamed round at the big house and the silent servants. He went up to Heeun. We watched, but she did extremely well. She didn't turn into a flailing mess like I would have. She kept this incredibly charming smile on her face and she kept giggling with her hand over her mouth, and nodding, and shaking her head, and it was a wonderful mime. You didn't even have to hear her to know what she was saying, 'Yes … yes … great idea! .. but impossible … sorry … impossible … so sorry …' so J.P. had to walk away empty-handed and not even able to jeer at her. You couldn't jeer at those giggles. He went up to Celine and draped his arm round her and soon they were necking in the corner. He generally necks Celine, but not always. She isn't his girlfriend. He doesn't have girlfriends. He moves around.

Well that kicked off necking time. Soon the usual couples were draped round the place. Anna sloped off with Carl. I went up to Heeun. She was looking happy and I could see why because it was a successful party. Soon as J.P. arrived it was guaranteed success.

She said, 'Oh. Ben's turn for music.'

I looked and he was actually dancing like crazy to Michael Jackson. So I said, 'Let's wait till he notices.'

She said, 'Yes, because I think if we start pogo-ing, someone

will be injured' and we giggled. I was looking round for David Leydon though. He hadn't arrived. I don't know who Heeun was looking round for. I hadn't asked her.

Then after a bit Ben came up to Heeun, and said, 'Hey, my go on the decks now' and she smiled and said, 'Yes, Ben' and went up and he changed places with Caroline and her friends and soon we were all leaping about totally unrhythmically, but with loads of energy and it was mad fun.

Heeun's method was working brilliantly. We'd been getting sick of Caroline's pop dance tunes, we wanted something mental.

So there I was chucking myself round the floor and bumping – *bang!* – deliberately into Ben so he'd send me flying – *bang!* – into Pierce (very brave of me!) and even J.P. had laid off necking Celine to join in the scrum – boom! boom! boom! – and all of us leaping and sweating like crazy, when I saw come in the door David Leydon and Derek and Brian and that guy, Hallowe'en Boy – Keith – that we'd met in town that day party shopping. So my heart leapt and I thought *great!* and kept on jumping about but keeping an eye on them and I saw they surrendered immediately to the wild atmos and flung their coats on the floor so they could join in. Even David Leydon did and he is usually a stand-offish kind of a person.

At that moment Anna came up and shouted in my ear, 'I've broken up with Carl!'

I shouted back, 'Oh!' and then, 'Why?' and she shouted, 'I'm fed up of him!'

I could think of a lot of things to say but I just yelled sarcastically, 'Well, this makes a change!' and she looked a tiny bit cross, but then she began to laugh because, really she had to admit, *what* change did it make? I guess she had to break up with him in a party because that's the only time she speaks to him. So then I went *thud* into her and sent her flying and then I saw J.P. go *thud* into her and I was jealous, of course I was. Imagine being flung into the middle of next week by J.P.!

But then – *bang!* – I was sent flying by Derek and – *bang!* – I sent myself flying into David Leydon, and now the dancefloor was actually getting dangerous because with David and the others there were far more boys on it than girls and nobody was holding back and the good thing was at least I was wearing Doc Martens not ballet slippers because all the girls in ballet slippers had had to retreat for fear of getting their feet stamped and then I saw Anna was on J.P.'s shoulders! His white t-shirt was drenched with sweat. If she put her hands down she could have felt his greasy hair, but she was waving them in the air, and he was rocking her about, and then – *wooah* – I felt myself lifted up, up and I was on Pierce's shoulders which if not very exciting shoulders to be on were at least *safe* shoulders, being so wide, and we were rocking up and down and going – *thud* – into J.P. and Anna, and I was pushing Anna as I thudded into her and we were having

hysterics laughing and then it was all the craze – J.P. had started it – the dancefloor was full of girls on boys' shoulders, and all the girls in ballet slippers were back in the game because now their feet were safe, and we were charging into each other. Heeun was on Ben's shoulders. But I checked – David Leydon didn't have anyone on his shoulders (good).

And then, just like that, we all calmed down. Which may have been because a) J.P. stopped and lowered Anna to the floor, or b) the music changed and Ben put on something else which just didn't do it for us, or c) we were all exhausted, especially the boys carrying us, so we all went off to get beer (J.P.) and coke (the rest of us).

Straight off David Leydon and Derek and Keith came over to me and Anna, and Keith said, 'Cool party,' and Derek said, 'Yeah, where's the parents?'

We chatted on like that. Keith was definitely chatting Anna up, it was like when we met in town, but much more obvious. Then Ben put on 'Smells Like Teen Spirit' which is an All Time Classic and we wanted to dance to that and we'd cooled down by now so we hit the dance floor and jumped around. There were a lot of people jumping round but I couldn't see J.P. anywhere.

After a bit I saw Myung – the nanny/housekeeper/pseudo mum – was talking intently to Heeun and Heeun was looking quite upset so I went over.

Heeun said, 'Oh Denise …' and then quietly, 'Myung has had to throw J.P. out.'

I said, 'Oh my God! Why?'

Heeun said, 'He was upstairs in the salon, going through the cabinets.'

My jaw dropped open. I was totally totally shocked. This was an unbelievable way to behave. Stealing! And it didn't seem like J.P. He's up for it, for fun I mean, but he's not like a criminal. And then, suddenly I knew, 'He was looking for booze,' I said in relief, 'not stealing!'

Heeun looked confused.

'Drink,' I explained, in case booze was not a word that people in Korea used, 'he was looking for your dad's beer or whiskey or something. He wasn't trying to steal your precious ornaments!'

She said 'Oh,' and started speaking Korean to Myung. It sounds a very strange language.

Heeun turned back to me, 'Myung says it is still stealing … and he is too young to be drinking *booze*.'

'Right,' I said, 'Myung is right, but …' I turned to her 'Of course you had to throw him out,' I said earnestly, 'but looking for booze is not the same as stealing, really it's not, I mean you don't have to call the police or anything!'

I must have looked incredibly worried and this must have looked incredibly stupid – the combination of my worried face with my punky hair maybe – because suddenly Myung started to giggle and then Heeun caught on and they were both giggling at me.

'Oh Denise,' said Heeun, 'of course we aren't going to call the police!' and 'The *police!*' said Myung, going off into peals, as if I'd suggested calling in Darth Vader's storm troopers, so then I began to giggle too, though I didn't know why.

Heeun said, 'Myung is not even going to tell my parents, right?' and she looked pleading/super charmingly at Myung but Myung said, 'Oh yes, so sorry, must tell your parents,' and Heeun sighed but didn't argue it.

I went back to the dancefloor where by now there were excited huddles, saying; 'J.P!' – the word had got round. The most excited was clustered round Celine who was looking tearful and righteous and self-important. I looked round to tell Anna and I couldn't see her. I couldn't see her anywhere. And I couldn't see Keith either!

And then Derek came up and we chatted for a bit about J.P. and Derek said thoughtfully, 'It's not really on to steal from your friends' parents', so I said, 'No, but obviously you could if they *weren't* your friends!' and he got that I was being sarcastic and laughed. When he'd finished laughing, he gulped and said, 'Do you want to come outside?'

I said, 'What?' He said, 'Outside. Do you want to come outside?'

I was thinking, *hmm, outside, okay, see the gardens, probably Heeun has big gardens,* but there was something about the way he was asking … nervous or something … and then he said, 'Anna

and Keith have gone outside' and I looked up and his enthusiastic dark-brown eyes were shining hopefully at me like I was going to let him play a great game, so *then* I got it, and I acted totally instinctively.

I said, 'I've just got to sort something for Heeun,' and I moved off, really fast, leaving him standing there.

My heart was beating very fast. *Derek* wanted me to go outside with him! I had no idea of this. Shouldn't you have an idea? I had never even thought about him like that. I hardly thought about him at all. He did not give me a shivery dreadful feeling like Carl, and he did not give me excited goosebumps like J.P., he did not make me feel irritated and cruel like Declan did, and he did not intrigue me like David Leydon … the only thing he made me feel was friendly. I didn't want his shiny enthusiastic eyes to turn sad, that's all. I was glad I hadn't looked at them when I moved off.

Oh, where was David Leydon? Was he asking a girl to come outside?? I looked around and he was leaning against the wall, shoulders slumped, so I went over and said, 'Hey. Have you heard about J.P?'

He said, 'Uh-huh. Stupid him getting caught.'

I said, 'Yeah!' but somewhere inside I did not like this remark – it was a kind of a try-hard remark. I started telling him about how I'd been afraid they'd call the police, but they weren't going to, and he was nodding, and we were having a conversation,

definitely, but that's all it was. He never moved from his (admittedly cool but also try-hard) stance leaning against the wall, and he never really volunteered any information. He just reacted to what I said. As usual. Which gets exhausting. There was no chance of him asking me (or anyone else I didn't think) outside.

Luckily I was rescued from this actually quite desperate situation. I looked up and two new adults had come in and were talking to Heeun. They were very well-dressed.

'Oh,' I said, 'Heeun's parents. I'd better say hello.' So David Leydon just stared ahead with his usual unimpressed expression and probably he was thinking, 'whatever' in disgust at my creeping up to parents, but I was staying in their house and Heeun needed some help with the J.P. situation and anyway I was done standing and babbling to David Leydon, so up I went to be introduced. Heeun's mother was really pretty and seemed nice too. Her father was a bit scary. He looked like he'd be impossible to talk to. They looked around and they looked a bit confused and for a moment I saw the party through their eyes, all these kids, some of them very strangely dressed, jumping around to totally unrhythmic music. Probably they'd thought all the girls would be in pretty dresses like Heeun and all the boys would be in … chinos (or something ambassador-like) and we'd be doing ballroom dancing (or something ambassador-like).

Anyway then after a bit the other parents began to arrive, and people were leaving and soon it was just me and Anna and

Heeun. But I like the end of parties. We made some toasted sandwiches and we had a lot to talk about. I said to Anna, 'so is Keith your new boyfriend then?' She said, 'Maybe…' I told them about Derek. I didn't necessarily want to. I quite like keeping things like that to myself but I had to have something to tell them. Heeun said, 'Oh Denise! But he is quite hunky, I think.' So then Anna and I got such laughing fits we choked over our sandwiches – *hunky*, where the hell had she got that word? When we calmed down, I said, 'I dunno what I think about him.' Anna said, 'well maybe you should give it a try.' That is her philosophy, for sure. Like I said, she is pragmatic and unromantic, and ready to experiment. But I am romantic and I wonder – is there any point kissing someone if they don't give you goosebumps?

Phheww! My hand is exhausted from writing all that. It is a pretty comprehensive account. So now I have to think what to write on the blog. Not a comprehensive account, and not tonight anyway …

TUESDAY DECEMBER 1ST

The boys *do* all fancy Heeun! It is going round the class. I don't why it took them so long to realise this. Maybe she is a slow-burner, not like Celine who was an instant hit? Or maybe when they saw her in her very pretty dress in her very big house, they realised they all fancied her? I don't know, but anyway, they know now. So as a result Caroline Hunter is all over Heeun. But

since me and Anna got to her first, Heeun has no time for Caroline Hunter. She (Heeun) is being (typically) modest about all this attention. Probably now she can go out with any boy she wants to (except J.P. – because he doesn't go out with people, and somehow I think that she is not his type).

We went back to Heeun's to write the blog. We couldn't write it in Anna's because of being rumbled, and obviously I'd prefer to go to Heeun's then mine. Heeun's is cool; there is loads of delicious food, and it is so big and tidy, it makes you feel light and floating. We have let Heeun in on the blog, seeing as she is our friend. Of course there were more notices posted up today and some of them were quite menacing.

Pippa:

It's only a party girls, get over it, get out of bed, and fill us in.

ZeeZee:

So what? Spill the beans. How bad can it be? So – oooh! – you kissed someone's toe?

(Weird! Why *toe*?)

Others were kinder:

Come on, we're all agog ...

CuriousinDenver

but all were insistent.

Heeun giggled, 'Oh, they are like teachers looking for homework!' This was somehow a quite cute image.

'Like vampires, more like,' said Anna darkly, 'sucking our

blood ...' but we thought we'd better give them what they wanted to shut them up. So this is what we wrote:

Sorry for not updating you. Truly we were exhausted and also we had to do more community service on Sunday (remember that?)

So the party was in our friend Hefto's house

[blurred photo of Heeun. Anna and I think it's *hysterical* that Heeun's predictive-text name is 'Hefto'. You can't imagine anyone less hefty!]

and it was pretty mental

[photo of the dance floor which Anna had taken with her phone from J.P.'s shoulders so it was the tops of people's heads, pretty cool!]

Demise looked punk

[photo we took of back of my head with its punky hair]

and Hefto looked angelic

[photo of Heeun's dress, just the skirt bit]

and Bomb looked just exactly the same as usual!

[photo of Anna's runners].

Somebody got chucked out for trying to nick Hefto's parents' booze! Bomb dumped her boy-friend and got another! (She is a bombshell!) Demise refused all offers (She is hastening her own demise!) And Hefto is the new class pin-up! (but she hasn't decided who to pin

herself to…)

This showed how much trouble we'd gone to – all those photos, which we took in advance for the express purpose of uploading them (that's preparation!) – so perhaps it will keep our readers quiet for a bit. And luckily (well, it wasn't luck – I made sure) we did not mention the servants. That could incite a riot among our right-on, power-to-the-people readers!

WEDNESDAY DECEMBER 2ND

Went to chat to David Leydon and Brian and Derek today. I thought I'd better behave very naturally in case Derek was embarrassed, although luckily I hadn't exactly rejected him because he hadn't exactly asked me (although as good as). He did look just a bit embarrassed but I kept chatting until he relaxed, and soon his eyes went from mortified to enthusiastic, and we were talking friendly as ever. This is not always the case, I know, because I've heard Renata and Alva in Anna's kitchen talking about guys they've rejected – Alva (scornfully): 'And now he's cold-shouldering me, as if I've *mortally* offended him' – Renata: 'Yeah, like get over it, I don't fancy you, live with it.'

While I was chatting away normally, I was taking sneaky secret looks at Derek, seeing him in a new way. His skin is quite good for a boy's, less spotty than David Leydon's (although who knows what's under that greasy fringe?!), and he is tall enough and although his arms obviously can't compare to J.P's, they are

quite wiry and muscular (I obviously have a thing for arms!). But I wasn't getting goosebumps, unfortunately. David Leydon was moody and silent as usual. I think he would like to be too cool for school but sorry, Dave, it takes more than black clothes and moodiness to be too cool for school. And as soon as you *try*, you aren't, you know. So you either are or you aren't, live with it! I mean J.P does not wear black (any time I see him outside school he is wearing very tight light-blue jeans and a grey sweater – and that's what he was wearing at the party) and he is not that moody (although I think he has a temper, I mean sometimes he punches people – boys, I mean. He does not have a temper around girls).

THURSDAY DECEMBER 3RD

On the blog:

Xena:

way to go girls! A tease, a fast-mover and a pin-up! Dynamite combination!

I worked out who was who and it seemed I was the tease because Anna was definitely the fast mover. I didn't really see how I'd been teasing, like I never mentioned any practical jokes or jeering, but I thought it might mean something else the way words do, so I texted Anna:

check clog. What's a tease? Ask Senata

She texted back:

a flirt. Someone who makes it seen like she'll song

the guy, then doesn't.

I unscrambled 'song' – it means snog.

I thought that was pretty unfair of Xena! I never ever made it seem like I'd song Derek, no way! And I don't make it seem like I'd song Declan either! (Why do all my admirers have to begin with 'De' – I should go in search of a cute Dean, or a Dermot, or a Dexy, or maybe I'd better just start saying DEvid Leydon (*ha!*))

Well at least I *hope* I don't make it seem like I'd song. But maybe I do? How do you make it seem like you'd song anyway? If I don't know *how* than maybe I do it unconsciously?

This is A Concern.

But I defended myself. I wrote on the blog:

I (Demise) am no tease! I do not ever imply that I will song the guy. It is really not my fault if they get that impression!

SATURDAY 5TH DECEMBER

Went into town with Anna to meet Keith. I said, why did I have to come? She said just *because* … so I brought Heeun. Luckily, because Keith arrived by himself, so it would have been just me and the Happy Couple. He looked confused and not that happy to see me and Heeun, but he got over that quickly and began to take charge. He always has to be the leader in any group he's in, I think. So does Anna really, so this is gonna be a problem for them, unless they take it in turns … For today while we were

with them, she let Keith take charge, maybe because she had me and Heeun, so she thought he needed something.

Keith knows a lot of stuff and he likes to talk. I think once he got over being annoyed he was glad me and Heeun were there because he had three girls to look at him and listen to him and giggle at his jokes. But after burgers me and Heeun said we had to go and we left them to it. We went round shops. Dunno where they went.

Heeun said cheerfully, 'He seems nice!'

I said, 'Yeah… if you like listening!'

So then she giggled and said, 'I don't think Anna is a number one listener …'

I am finding out that you have to prod Heeun. Her first reaction is always to say something nice and sweet, but if you prod her a bit, she says what she really thinks, which is not necessarily nice and sweet …

Did some Christmas shopping. Heeun has something like a million pounds to spend on presents. I brought Justine an Alice band. I think it will suit her.

Later

Have just remembered – Anna did not go and help Asylum seekers today! Neither did I go to soup kitchen (have decided it is just for Sundays, like mass) but I do not claim to be as committed as Anna. Her social conscience is being corrupted by sex!

SUNDAY 6TH DECEMBER

Suspect Heeun has as big a social conscience as Anna. Well, at least, she is religious. She had a very religious conversation, all about mass, to Agnes. She is making a very good impression in the soup kitchen. She is a very neat chopper – all her carrots are chopped the same size, in perfect little matchsticks. It is quite amazing, as if a machine had gone through them. Mine are all sizes and all shapes. I am quite jealous of her chopping skills – it came to me as I sat there hacking off great, ugly, shredded chunks of carrot, that Heeun's carrots are like her hair and clothes, and my carrots are like *my* hair and clothes …

Mr Noisy shouted at us today, 'God loves every hair on your head!' We looked at each other, and then, at exactly the same time, we both put our hands to our heads and twiddled our hair, to check what it is God loves … it is nice that He loves messy hair like mine exactly the same as neat hair like Heeun's.

MONDAY 7TH DECEMBER

I asked Anna if she was in love with Keith. She was nonchalant and off-handish about it, actually very similar to how she was over Carl, so I'm guessing this is not love either, but more pragmatism, although it's *improved* pragmatism because Keith is a step up from Carl, and is not that bad really. I mean he's an energetic and chatty person with initiative. It's just a pity he's a bit of

a know-it-all and a bit, I dunno … in his head. What do I mean by that? Well I think I mean he is ruled by his head – when you think of him you see his head and his mouth talking. Whereas some other people are in their bodies – J.P. definitely, when you think of him you see his veiny arms and his tight jeans with his hands scrunched into his pockets. And Tommy too, when he's on stage he's fluid and it's like his head is just another part of his body, not necessarily the most important part. And even David Leydon, if I think of him I see him leaning against a wall, his long back and his moody, slumpy shoulders.

So now I know what J.P. and Tommy and David Leydon have in common (because otherwise they've nothing in common!)

I was curious though. Why doesn't Anna kiss J.P.? If I got an electric charge from him like she does, I definitely would. But I didn't ask her because I didn't want to plant the idea in her head, because if she did get to kiss J.P., I might explode from jealousy. Sorry, it's not that I don't want my best friend to be happy and not go up in life and improve on Carl and Keith, but let's not go too far! Like I've already said I am not an actual do-gooder. Besides she didn't need me to put the idea in her head, I mean if *I* can feel the electric charge, so can she. I guess it's that she knows that J.P. wouldn't actually go out with her, wouldn't be the pragmatic boyfriend that you could use when you needed him. J.P. would be trouble.

TUESDAY 8TH DECEMBER

Heeun wants to know what animal she is so she can put it up on the blog. We said we'd have to ask Renata because she is the (nasty) expert on this, so after school we all went round to Anna's. This time all the Lotto numbers came up (except her Dad obviously; it was too early). Even Alva was there. Heeun looked all open-eyed and excited, just like me the first time I was ever in Anna's kitchen. I hope she doesn't take my place. This is a very real concern.

After a bit we said to Renata, 'So what animal is Heeun like?'

Renata didn't miss a beat. She said, 'Butterfly'.

We said, *'Butterfly?'*

'Yeah, because she's shy and everything about her flutters. You know – her eyelashes, and her giggles and her hands fluttering up to her mouth … and she flies down to sit on your finger and then she flies away again,' Renata looked assessingly at Heeun in her uniform, 'And probably she wears bright colours …'

Heeun cried, 'But I want to be a St Bernard!' so then we all exploded laughing (Tommy and Anna's mum too) because you couldn't imagine anyone less like a St Bernard. It is amazing how people's idea of themselves is so far from what they are. 'Yes!' said Heeun, also laughing, but also earnest, wanting to be taken seriously, 'very loyal, and hard-working and useful, and saving

people's lives!'

I looked at her closer then, and I could see that actually she is very loyal and hard-working and useful and would like to save people's lives, but … sorry, Heeun, you definitely look like a butterfly. And she does wear bright colours when she's out of her school uniform! And she is always flying away – I mean she has been to four schools in four different countries already. How did Renata know? That is the type of thing you know if you're a genius, I guess.

'Anyway,' I said, 'at least a butterfly is pretty, not like a frog and a chipmunk!'

'Yes,' said Renata, 'you'd better watch out for lepidopterists.' Then, because we were looking at her incomprehensibly (obviously!), 'A lepidopterist is a butterfly-collector. Only stamps inspire the same obsession from collectors as butterflies. Yes' (dreamily) 'they'll want to catch you and drop a drop of ether on your head and pin you to a slide where they can look at you forever.'

Heeun looked terrified. Poor her. She is not used to Renata. Me and Anna waited, and sure enough:

'Oh, Renata!' said her mother.

WEDNESDAY 9TH DECEMBER

Got picture of butterfly and put it up on the blog with:

    animal Hefto resembles.

The blog has a load more comments all spinning from my last entry:

Xenawarriorcleaner:

what's songing???!!

(Then I realised that I written in 'song' instead of 'snog' – didn't mean to!)

Pippa wrote:

Yeah!! Is this some bizarre dating ritual that hasn't come to Ohio yet?

CuriousinDenver:

Don't worry Demise! I'm sure you would never imply that you'd song. I'm sure you don't even *think* about songing!

ZeeZee:

Yeah. But bet Bomb songs like crazy!

Eloise at the Holiday Inn:

And Hefto heaves ho!

We all looked at each other. Heeun said, 'what is songing?' So we explained about predictive texting. And then we were all laughing but also, you know, kind of alarmed. Well it is alarming having all these strangers commenting on everything you write. I mean suddenly you've all these shrieking voices in your living room, all having a laugh and making jokes at your expense.

I said, 'God, it's like giving Renata a portal into your brain.'

So Anna cracked up, and Heeun too cause now she knows what Renata's like.

We confab-ed on what to reply. This is what we posted up:

Oh ha *ha!* A song is just a snog is just a French kiss... Sorry, it's not that bizarre, it's no ritual and I guess you do it too!

Demise has so *thought* about songing ...

Bomb is (quite) liking her new boyfriend.

Hefto has not pinned herself to anyone yet. She is afraid a lepidopterist will catch her and pin her to a slide!

God loves every hair on your head!

THURSDAY 10TH DECEMBER

You're coasting along and everything's okay, and the trouble's over and you think you've learnt something and that's when – *bang!* – the real trouble hits.

This is bad, bad trouble, worse than the racist stickers, and I don't know what to do.

I am sitting in my bedroom and I've been sitting here twenty minutes looking mindlessly out the window. I am not crying. I am in numbed shock.

I don't know what to do.

I came home – just half an hour ago! Imagine! Thirty-five minutes ago everything was fine – I was a bit late back 'cause I'd

gone to Anna's after school and delayed a bit, but I wasn't actually late for dinner or anything. The house was quiet, but when I went into the kitchen Mum was sitting at the table, and she was just gazing ahead like me now, and something about the way she was sitting and gazing – because normally she's always busy – made me say, 'Are you alright Mum?'

She said, still gazing ahead, 'It's Justine.'

I said, 'Justine?'

She said, 'She's—'

But I can't write what Mum said Justine is. I can't! It's too terrifying. It's a scary, scary word.

I said, 'No, she's not!' but in a reflex way. I didn't even think about it. I just denied it.

Mum said harshly, 'You know she is. When did you last see her eat her dinner?'

I thought about it. I never notice what Justine does, but now Mum said it, it came to me, Justine sitting miserably at dinner turning the food round with her fork on the plate, and all of it staying on the plate, not going to her mouth.

I said feebly (and desperately), 'Maybe she fills up before dinner? On cereal! When she gets in from school.'

Mum said, 'The cereal's never touched.' She was still gazing flatly ahead.

I said wildly, 'I'll – I'll talk to her, I'll see what's going on. I'll make sure she eats. I'll–'

'You?' Mum took her horrible, blank gaze from straight ahead and turned it on me, still blank, but now with a bit of scorn in it, 'You? What will *you* do? You don't care about anyone but yourself. You ignore your sister. You ignore your father and me. You spend every moment you can in Anna's house. When you do eat here, you make it clear it's a boring duty imposed on you. You snap and sulk. It's obvious you consider us dull and unworthy of your wit and humour. You devise complacent, self-congratulatory games with Anna, which involve being cruel to other kids. God help you, but you're a selfish little monster.'

I looked at her. A full five seconds we looked straight at each other, then I turned and ran up here.

Yes, she said all that, in just those words. I will never forget them. And first I raged and raged and thought, *she's trying to hurt me, she's just trying to hurt, because she's upset*, but I knew that wasn't it, I knew she really thought those things because of the dead blank way she said them, not like she planned them, but like they were coming from somewhere very deep inside her. Then I tried to defend myself. In my mind I tried to reject what she said, but I couldn't. How could I? My little sister is – and I didn't even know. I hardly even noticed she was miserable. How can I defend myself against that?

Well then I had evidence. I mean I had this diary, so I read back over all of it, from the beginning, and I burned, burned, *burned* with shame. Suddenly it was like one of those 3D pictures where

you think you're looking at a load of colourful shapes and then you adjust your eyes and suddenly a man on a horse (or whatever) emerges from the random shapes. Or maybe like when you read a book in English and you like the story but then you go through it with O'Toole and you pick up on all the hidden bits, and the Metaphors and the Allusions, and it seems a different book. I mean I've read over this diary before and giggled, because it seemed funny, very entertaining, but now my eyes are adjusted, now I'm looking for the hidden bits, the metaphors and allusions, and all I see is selfishness and me being totally rude and dismissive to my parents, and actually *cruel* to Justine. It's horrible. I want to rip the pages up.

I don't care about what we did to Jayne O'Keeffe. I said I was sorry but all those accusations of selfishness and bullying, they just bounced right off me, but now mum's words have slid in like a razor blade.

I don't know what to do – to make myself less selfish. Or (more important) to save Justine.

FRIDAY DECEMBER 11TH

We are going to speak to Justine. Tomorrow. 'We' is me and Anna.

At break Anna said, 'What's wrong?' She is a noticing kind of person, but also my behaviour was odd. Tense, I mean.

I said, 'Nothing,' in an aggressive, tense voice because I didn't

want to tell her. I thought she was part of the problem. She was part of me being so selfish.

She said, 'Come on,' then to Heeun (in a nice way), 'Do you mind? There is just something we have to straighten out,' and she took my arm and walked me down towards the bike sheds. She said, 'Now what is it?' in a very firm, direct way, not in a particularly sympathetic way but in a way that needs an answer.

I said, 'It's –' then I looked away from her, at the sky, and my eyes filled up with tears. I couldn't look at her. I was embarrassed and angry and ashamed. 'It's Justine' I said, 'Mum says she's –' and I said what Mum said she was.

Anna said, 'She's not!' in shock, and then I started to shout, totally unreasonably, about what would she know, and what was it to her, and all the rest. She just took it. She didn't shout back. She put her hand on my arm and said, 'I know she's not very happy …'

I said, '… and that's my fault! I'm a rotten sister!'

'No. You're just an *older* sister. Like Renata.'

'Like Renata?' and I didn't know whether this was good or bad because Renata is a total bitch to Anna, but on the other hand, she does love her, you can see that.

'Yes,' said Anna, 'like Renata. Justine annoys you, but you love her.' I hoped this was true. When I thought about it, I was worse than Renata. At least Renata makes jokes at Anna's expense. I just ignore Justine.

Well then Anna had me back on side a bit, so I told her everything, about how selfish I was (although I didn't say Mum's exact words, I will never ever repeat them to anyone though I will never ever forget them myself). Anna didn't say I wasn't selfish.

She said, 'Maybe we get carried away, like with Instruments of Karma, and we think something's fun when it's mean ...' And then she said, 'and I feel bad, cause I'm a younger sister and I *knew* Justine was miserable.'

So now everybody's feeling bad. Which is how it should be. If someone is miserable under your eyes and you do nothing about it, you *deserve* to feel bad.

We agreed that we would ask Justine did she want to come for chips and coke with us and we would find out then. We tried to find Justine after school to invite her this afternoon but we couldn't see her, so it will have to be tomorrow. I should be able to ask Justine alone, but I can't. Relations between us are so bad, I can't. I am ashamed of this.

But Anna is an amazing friend. If I am selfish, it is not her fault.

SATURDAY DECEMBER 12TH

So, Justine is NOT anorexic.

Now she is *not*, I can write it. (Though it is still a horrible word – just look at it. Look at that evil *x* and the sick kick of the *ic*).

She is being bullied. Being bullied stresses her so she loses her appetite, but she isn't actually trying to control her food intake or get thinner. This is how we found out:

Anna came round ours at lunchtime and we asked Justine did she want to come up to the shopping centre for chips and burgers. She looked amazed and suspicious, but she came.

I didn't know how we were going to approach this, what roundabout way we were going to lead up to it, but Anna is not roundabout, she is straight to the chase. Over the chips and burgers we just chatted about general things, then we got some sundaes and Justine seemed more relaxed.

Then Anna said, 'The reason we invited you out is that we're afraid something's bothering you.'

Justine said, 'Bothering me?'

'Yeah,' said Anna, 'Look, I'm a younger sister so I kind of know how younger sisters feel and it seems to me something's bothering you. Before I came to this school, *I* was miserable.'

'You were?' said me and Justine at the same time.

'Yeah, because there was this bitch in my class, and she was just bullying me …'

'You too?' said Justine, and that was it. I wanted to exchange a look with Anna, but I didn't, we both just looked at Justine, but in a casual, relaxed way because we didn't want to scare her off. It was like trying to get a cat to take food from your fingers. But then it all came out, in kind of fits and jerks, like Justine was

embarrassed about it (which of course she is).

Who is mostly bullying her is Jayne O'Keeffe.

When I heard that I went nuts. I forgot about being relaxed and not insistent. I shouted,

'That little *cow!*' and then, 'I can't believe we *apologised* to her! I'm gonna wring her *neck!*'

So then Anna and Justine exchanged a look and Anna said, 'Calm down Denise,' but Justine looked quite pleased. Then Anna said, 'Did that make it worse for you, when we apologised?'

Justine looked at her plate, she said, 'Yeah, well it did, she said *I* had to be punished for my sister spreading lies about her ... She didn't dare say anything to Gita after all the fuss, so she just took it out on me ...'

I let out an awful groan, and Anna grabbed Justine's arm and said, 'Oh no! *Sorry!*'

Then I said, 'Why didn't you *tell* us?' and Justine said, 'Because ...' So I didn't press her because there were only two possible answers and both of them were equally depressing – she didn't tell me because a) we weren't speaking to each other, and/or b) she thought I wouldn't care.

Well then we had an emotional time. We ordered more sundaes and we all exchanged stories about Bad Times. Anna said about the girl who was bullying her in primary school – it all started because Anna didn't have a TV so she didn't know what

were the programmes everyone was talking about. So I said shouldn't she have told her mum and *forced* her to get a TV, and Anna said she was too embarrassed to tell her. Then Justine said *exactly*, that's why she never said ... (But all the same I can't imagine anyone bullying Anna and I think that maybe she is exaggerating this story in order to relate to Justine's problems). So then I said how I didn't have real friends, just virtual and default friends, until I met Anna (which was not entirely true either because in kindergarten I was fixated on a girl called Siobhan MacMahon, but it was true enough, and helped me to relate). And then we started thinking what to do about the bullying, and I was all for just bashing Jayne O'Keeffe, but Justine said *No-oo!* and by that time we were emotionally wrecked, like someone had squeezed us in the middle, so we agreed to all have a think and come back to it tomorrow.

And then as we were getting up to go, I said awkwardly, 'Sorry Justine, sorry I wasn't there for you.' I don't at all like saying sorry, but it had to be done.

She said (also awkwardly), 'Oh, that's ok ...' and Anna beamed on us.

SUNDAY DECEMBER 13TH

It isn't okay though, it's awful. Yesterday I was so relieved about the anorexia that bullying seemed quite minor, but then I had a horrible dream with people jeering at me all the way through it,

and then I remembered how miserable I was when I fought with Anna and that only lasted a few days. Justine's been going months and months – not just without a friend, but with actual enemies.

I really do want to kill Jayne O'Keeffe. It is only Anna and Justine restraining me.

And I got worried in school.

I asked Anna, 'How do we know she's not anorexic? Maybe she's been bullied *and* is anorexic.'

Anna said, 'No, because she ate her ice-cream. She didn't finish her burger, but she ate *both* ice-creams. And they're very fattening. And she ate her second ice-cream very fast and with relief because by then we'd started discussing bullying which meant everything was out in the open and she was relaxing. That's why – when I saw her eating ice-cream, I thought probably she isn't anorexic because an anorexic person wouldn't wolf down something so fattening. When Renata's stressed, she doesn't eat, so I thought it might be the same with Justine, that she's stressed, not anorexic ...'

This was very observant of Anna.

It also explains why Renata is so thin.

We still haven't decided what to do about Jayne O'Keeffe. We had all kinds of ideas. Then Anna said we should ask her mum. I think she's right. I mean her mum can psycho-analyse the situation.

But that will have to wait till tomorrow, because first I had to get back home to *my* mum. I needed to get her alone. I had to do one nice thing and one hard thing. First (nice thing) explain that Justine is not anorexic, but bullied; and second (hard thing) say sorry for being so selfish.

Well if you think my mum said, *oh thank you darling, and you're not really selfish*, then you don't know my mum. She just said all right, and she was sure I'd try harder. But she was very very relieved about Justine, although she said we needed to keep an eye on her eating anyway. And then we had a hug.

But of course now *she* is thinking what to do about the bullying. She wants to tell the teachers. I guess that is the typical parent reaction. Telling the teachers is not what came into my head.

MONDAY DECEMBER 14TH

Round to Anna's with Heeun. We decided to let Heeun in on this because a) to leave her out would be hurtful and actually quite like bullying and b) she is very discreet and is definitely not going to tell anyone.

So we began to tell Anna's mum in the kitchen, and when we got to the bit about who was doing the bullying, I said, 'Jayne O'Keeffe!' and Anna's mum said, 'The girl whose back you stuck the sticker on?' and I said, '*yes!*' and she just said, 'oh dear' quietly, but Renata said 'Jesus! You two are like the government – lurching from one crisis to another.' Anna's mum said, '*Renata!*

(much quicker than usual), and then, 'If you can't say anything helpful you'd better leave.'

So Renata said, 'Sorry,' and Anna and me looked at each other, amazed, because this was a first, but actually I didn't mind Renata being snide. It made me feel more normal.

So then we all started on what to do. Surprisingly Renata agreed with me – she said a good thump was what Jayne O'Keeffe needed.

Her mother said, *ye-es*, but that Anna and I had to be careful, we were already in trouble over Jayne O'Keeffe once. If we went and thumped her, and she told a teacher, then we'd be in *serious* trouble. This is a Good Point. In fact, unfortunately, it is an Indisputable Point. Anna's mum, like my mum, thinks bullying is something teachers have to sort out, but Renata said, 'Oh *mum!* But they never *can* sort it out. I mean she'll just get the silent treatment.'

Her mum said that was better than being actually mocked, but that yes of course, being ostracised was no solution really. Then she said what she was concerned about was Justine's self-esteem, and Heeun said in her earnest way, 'Yes, most important is for her to feel good about herself.'

Anna's mum said in a kind of teacher-y way, 'Exactly. And what are the ways we feel good about ourselves?'

And I said, 'When we have real friends, not just default friends.'

Renata murmured, 'Default friends' in an appreciating voice (which means she thinks that's a clever concept!) and Anna's mum said kindly, 'Yes, exactly, but unfortunately, we cannot just produce real friends for her, that is something she'll have to do herself.'

Then Heeun said, 'If she did something very well, she'd feel good about herself.'

'Yeah,' said Anna, 'but she has to be *seen* to be doing it very well and it has to be a cool thing – I mean there's no point her being very good at … chopping carrots if nobody sees her doing it, and nobody thinks it's a cool thing to be good at.' So we all laughed, especially me, cause Anna got chopping carrots from my soup kitchen for sure.

'So what's she good at?' said Renata.

I thought and I couldn't think of anything, and this was humiliating. I mean she has to be good at something and I should know what it is. All I could think of was the fact that she was good at playing doll's houses when we were small, and that she does have a quiet sense of humour, but I couldn't see how to turn that into anything.

'Sport? Gymnastics?' said Heeun anxiously. I shook my head. Justine is about as athletic as piece of wood.

'No,' I said, 'and she's not good at schoolwork either, so don't ask.'

'Being good at school work doesn't stop you being bullied anyway,' said Anna.

'Art? Music?' said Renata.

'No,' I said, because she never draws and she can't play an instrument, but then I remembered, 'oh, she does have quite a good voice.'

'*Quite* good, or very good?' said Renata.

'Well, it's sweet,' I said, 'and in tune. It's not a big voice but it sounds … nice, sweet.'

We all thought about that. 'Maybe she could join the school choir?' said Anna's mum. But we all shook our heads because that would take ages – she'd have to do trials and then she'd just be stuck in the chorus for ages, and nobody would notice her, and nobody really thinks the choir is cool anyway.

And then Anna said, 'Oh I know … *Tommy!*'

TUESDAY DECEMBER 15TH

The main thing I'm working on is being nice to Justine, because Anna's mum said (and I knew anyway) that more important than revenge on the bullies was her having positive things in her life and stuff to look forward to.

But the thing is – I'll only admit it here – she is still a bit annoying. Sorry to say. But I guess this is not surprising because a) her being annoying isn't going to disappear overnight just because I'm hoping and *willing* it too, and b) Anna still annoys Renata, it's obvious. So it is possible to have a relationship with someone who annoys you.

(Although if I think about it Anna and Renata's relationship is hardly The Ideal. I mean Renata is witty, but she's hardly kind. I am working on being kind.)

Also because of what Mum said about me ignoring her and Dad and thinking my house is dull and unworthy, I have decided to make more effort to spend time here. So today I invited Heeun back. Of course Heeun is truly kind so I could see Justine adoring her.

This is part of what's (a bit) annoying, but I am (trying to) restrain these thoughts.

Anyway Heeun thinks I am very lucky to have a sister and a dad who comes home for dinner.

WEDNESDAY DECEMBER 16TH

Oh God – we have two parties to organise for this weekend! Christmas parties! On top of everything else we have to do!

Not to mention the soup kitchen and the asylum-seekers!

We have decided to go to them first and then do the party. This might well kill us with tiredness, but Heeun is gonna help with the party, so that's good. Of course we will get less money because we will have to divide in three but since we have two parties, that's covered. Besides, better less money than complete meltdown …

Thought I'd better check in on the blog. Although they seem to get on fine without us. I mean they're having a good time

arguing among themselves.

Sample of what's on blog:

CuriousinDenver:

Yeah, Hefto, beware of lepidopterists… are you a rare speciman?

ZeeZee:

Alright snoggers – birds do it, bees do it, even monkeys in their trees do it …

Girlgonecrazy:

Demise, Bomb and Hefto, I am new to your blog, but I think it rocks…

Hirhito:

God bless you too!

Tash:

But I'm bald! Does He love every non-hirsute follicle on my head?

CuriousinDenver:

Don't be facetious!!!

The more recent messages were getting demanding though:

Hirohito:

Next instalment please!

Pippa:

What about the asylum seekers and the soup kitchen? Can't you lot lay off songing for a bit and think of other people?

I wrote:

Oh, so sorry, Tash, no! — He only loves hair!

(This was mean but obviously Tash isn't really bald so it doesn't matter)

And:

Actually to be pedantic — birds and bees *don't* do it! Only we humans actually kiss! (aa-hh! Sweet!!).

(I did actually find this quite touching when I thought about it.)

Well that was fine, but just reactive, as Ms Jackson (our chemistry teacher would say). I was just reacting to their comments. I did really really want to put up the latest bullying instalment, but obviously it wouldn't have been fair. I mean possibly someone in our school might read it one day (other than Declan). I tried to write it up cryptically but it wasn't really working, or else I was paranoid, I was imagining people reading between the lines, so I decided to just write nothing. I might write it up if our plans come off.

What plans?

Well they are top secret so I am not even gonna reveal them here!

THURSDAY DECEMBER 17TH

Am trying to instil Justine with courage and reassure her, but she doesn't seem to need it – she is weirdly relaxed and nonchalant. I

hope this is not just false courage (but I'm afraid it is). She's eating a lot better though. She doesn't have a huge appetite but it's now on the normal scale. Even though her school situation hasn't really improved (yet!), just the fact that she has me and Anna and Heeun to talk to has relaxed her a lot. This has relaxed my parents so dinner-times are a lot more pleasant.

SATURDAY DECEMBER 19TH

Well I dunno, is there something about us? I mean is it our karma to sort out bullies? Has some bit of karma stuck to us and is it sending out signals so that we'll find ourselves in bullying situations for the rest of our lives? (Not quite sure how karma works). Because the poor little party girl today is being bullied. Mrs Sheilds (her mum) wanted us to come early and when we got there she told us she was having this Christmas party because Florabelle (her daughter) was being bullied. Her (Mrs Sheilds') policy was to befriend the bullies, and give them such a great time, so that they'd want to be friends with Florabelle and get invited back.

Heeun (earnestly), 'That is such a good idea, Mrs Shields.' (Mrs S beamed).

Anna (also earnestly), 'Do you have a television, Mrs Shields?' (Mrs S looked confused and said, 'Yes, we have two…' I watched Anna mentally tick off that reason).

I wanted to say (but didn't), 'Mrs Shields, does Florabelle

have a second name, like Jane or Sarah, that you could call her?'

But anyway she'd asked the right people to sort out the problem. We threw ourselves into that party as if it was the 1,500 metres and we were Olympic medalists. Yes, by the end of it we were actually panting and sweating and half dead from our exertions. Luckily the little girls were seven and little girls of seven really admire older girls especially when they are wearing sparkly earrings and shiny tops, like Heeun was.

I heard Florabelle saying nonchalantly to one girl, 'Yeah, they're my friends, they come and hang out with me a lot.'

I felt I should reassure Mrs S that her daughter was a perfect little liar who knew how to make the most of a situation and she'd be just fine. We played it up of course, hugging Florabelle as if she was our favourite teddy bear. She (Florabelle) seemed like a cool kid and I couldn't see why she was being bullied; but this just shows of course that bullying is pretty random (must tell Justine).

Bullies are not so random, however. Of course they are not all big hulking lumps like Pierce (who could model for a statue of A Bully, if anyone ever wanted to put up such a statue, which I can't imagine they would), but you can still spot them. I spotted the bullying ring-leader immediately; she was called Samantha and she wasn't a big hulking lump, she was a little curly thing, but she had a hard, nasty little face. So me and Heeun and Anna exchanged glances, and gave her a hard time, like in Pass the

Parcel, we said loudly 'Don't *hang* on to that parcel, Samantha, just pass it. Hanging on to it is really un-cool.'

Afterwards Mrs S thanked us profusely and Florabelle said did we want to come to their house in Clifden for New Year, and we said thanks, we just might (*Ha!* Mrs S looked kind of horrified at the idea – too bad, Mrs S, your plans are running away with you …)

We all felt pretty good about ourselves, cause we'd made money *and* helped a poor little bullied kid. The Instruments of Karma couldn't have done better (no, they'd have made a right mess of it, with their record!) But now I'm feeling guilty – I mean am I being complacent and self-congratulatory? Is that what mum would say? I am trying to be on the alert for this terrible trait within myself.

SUNDAY DECEMBER 20TH

Probably it is good to be so busy so I don't have to worry about next week. If I didn't have so much to do I'd be in my room chewing my nails and drawing spirals on the walls.

From the soup kitchen we had to leg it over to the party house. Well this was the exact reverse of yesterday's party because this time the party boy was the class bully! We caught him and a ferret-faced kid down the back of the garden pushing a puny kid against the wall. Our duties were torn – I mean we were getting paid to give the party boy a good time – but, hell, we're nothing if not the scourge of bullies, so Heeun took the puny kid by the

hand and said, 'Come with me, I've got a special treat for you.'

Then Anna said very briskly, 'Right, we can tell your parents or your teachers or you can take your punishment now, which is it to be?'

They said, 'We weren't doing *anything*', so I said, 'Okay, I'll just describe to Jake's parents how you were pushing him against the wall and they can decide if that was anything'.

So Birthday-boy whined, 'It's my *birthday*.'

So I said, 'I don't *think* birthdays mean you can bully whoever you want but I can check with your parents if you like.'

He said, 'No!'

Anna said, 'Because it's your birthday, we're giving you a chance to take your punishment now. Normally we'd just tell.'

They said, 'What is it?' in sulky voices, so Anna said 'Twelve press-ups.'

They laughed like that was easy, but they weren't used to Anna. She said 'straighten your backs ... no, all the way down ... lock your knees ... tuck in your arms ...' until they were puffing and panting and red-faced. Twelve proper press-ups is a lot for an eight-year-old boy. At the end they were cross and exhausted but laughing. There was quite a good-humoured atmosphere.

Anna said in a disgusted voice, 'God, you're *weak*. You need to build up your muscles, but not on other kids. If I hear you've been practising on other kids I'll—' and she drew her hand across her throat, 'but if I hear you've been good, I'll give you my

brother's chest-expander.'

When they ran off, quite happy, I said, 'Were we too nice?'

Anna said, 'I think it's better not to make a major issue of it. Bullies aren't necessarily bad at that age. They're bad at Jayne and Pierce's age. Anyway I've learnt that we can't eradicate bullying worldwide, we can just make sure it doesn't happen on our watch.'

She sounded sad and resigned. I was shocked, there's something scary about hearing Anna admit there's a social injustice she can't eradicate!

On the way home, Heeun said dramatically, 'Is nobody *normal*? Just having normal friendships?'

I said, '*We* are.'

Anna said, 'Nothing to be done. Bet there's bullying in Charlie's crèche.'

This seems a rather gloomy viewpoint.

Later

Well, at least I've something for the blog. I wrote up this weekend's party experiences and poured my heart out about the problem of The Bullies and The Bullied. It was pretty emotional. I am kind of regretting it now. Am not gonna write what I posted up because I don't know that I'll want to remember it in future years when I read over this diary. Oh alright then… one of my lines was: 'Is nobody *normal*? Are we condemned to play out, our

whole lives, the equally unattractive roles of Persecutor or Victim?'

You see what I mean?

Pretty heavy stuff.

Pretty pretentious too. And I don't even believe it. For example: me and Anna and Heeun are not persecuting each other; my dad and mum are not persecuting each other; Tommy and Declan are not persecuting each other ...

I could go on ...

I wonder is it cheating to take stuff down off the blog?

I am in an absolute *state* about Wednesday. How is Justine so calm?

MONDAY DECEMBER 21ST

Our readers are worried about me.

There were a lot of 'Cheer Up' and 'Relax' messages posted.

curiousinDenver wrote:

Demise, is Bomb bullying you? We know she's the boss of you - has this tipped over to persecution?

Xenawarrior cleaner:

You know you can phone the Samaritans anytime.

Oh God! Humiliation!

I wrote:

Thanks guys, I got a little bit stressed about things, but there is really no problem and Bomb is not even the boss of me, and certainly not bullying me. I am sorry for treating the blog like it is my personal sigh-chiatrist. I will tell you some jokes next time.

Well here is a joke now: what did the masochist say to the sadist? – 'Hit me!' – Sadist: 'No!'

I have a feeling that joke is gonna really get the readers going. Probably they will rush over to save me. But I couldn't resist it. I mean, I think it's funny.

TUESDAY DECEMBER 22ND

Sitting in my room gripping my hands into fists willing it to all turn out okay tomorrow.

Even Justine is (finally) worried. She didn't eat her dinner – i.e. she's stressed. Saw Mum looking upset (Justine has been eating okay since our talk). Wanted to reassure Mum but can't let on.

Of course I only have to do one thing tomorrow and it's the smallest of the three things.

Heeun has to do a hard thing.

And Justine has to do the hardest thing.

Anna doesn't have to do anything, but she is master-minding

our three-pronged attack, *and* running a stall.

THURSDAY DECEMBER 24TH

Christmas Eve!

God rest ye merry gentlemen and nothing you dismay …

So yesterday: The Most Momentous Day of Term:

I had the first task of the day. There weren't lessons really because it was the last day of term. In fact this day is dedicated to having fun and raising money for charity. We don't even have to wear our uniforms. Everyone makes a big effort to look good. There are athletics competitions – running, jumping and so on, but only for the best students. Most of the grounds are taken over by stalls selling food and hosting various games and competitions – like one stall has a wheel of fortune, you bet on what number is gonna come up, and at another stall you test your strength, pushing down on this weird contraption hung with weights. Mostly it's the kids who come up with the ideas for the stalls. If you have an idea you run it by the teachers, and if they like it, you get a stall and there's a kind of unspoken competition to see how much money you can raise. Well because it's the kids some of the stalls are quite way-out. Mostly it's the older kids who do the stalls, not us, and certainly not Justine's class, but we can get involved. Like this year there's a kissing stall! You pay money for a kiss! Well this was set up by the fifth years and they started off with Lucy Carter in the stall because she is recognised

as The Hottest Thing in School, but obviously she wasn't gonna sit there being kissed all day (although it is only a quick kiss, not a *song*) and also, said Joanne Dunne (who was organising it), you have to cater for all tastes (meaning that not absolutely *everybody* would fancy Lucy Carter). So other people took their turn. They even came to our class and asked who wanted to go in, so we all said (*sigh*): Celine.

But then I said, 'What about the boys?' and everyone laughed, including Joanne Dunne, who'd come to get kissing volunteers.

But Anna backed me up, 'Yeah,' she said, 'the boys have to be up for being kissed too! Otherwise it's sexist.'

There was practically a gasp – she'd used the *S* word! – and Joanne Dunne looked very nervous and very calculating all at once. So next we knew boys were being put up for the stall too, and that was thanks to me and Anna! They will raise twice as much money and it is all down to us!

Of course Tommy was immediately nominated, and he will be mobbed, poor him. Nobody put up J.P. – like I said people are just not honest about fancying him.

I am quite surprised the teachers allowed a kissing stall at all. Probably there was an argument about it in the Staff Room, but since there's no songing allowed, just the quickest peck on the lips, *and* it's for charity, it probably comes under the heading of Good, Clean Fun.

And of course – you've guessed – Anna had a stall. She was the

only person under third year to get a stall. She came up with a pretty neat idea: a fashion stall. People donate clothes they don't want and then we sell them on cheap. At the end of the day the left-over clothes (and the money of course) go to charity.

It was quite an unusual idea for Anna cause she doesn't exactly care about fashion. *Possibly* it was actually Renata's idea …

But back to my task! Before being released to spend the day wandering the stalls and giving up our money to charity, all the classes had to convene briefly with their form teacher. So we went to O'Toole's class and he gave us a short speech and wished us happy Christmas and said he'd see us after the holidays and then we all got up to go. But I lingered. He looked up when everyone had gone and saw I was still there and raised his eyebrows.

So I said, 'Mr O'Toole?' He nodded. 'In confidence.' He nodded. 'Well,' I said, 'the thing is, that girl, Jayne O'Keeffe—'

'Whom you wrongly accused?'

'Yeah, that girl, well the thing is, she *was* guilty of something …' He raised his eyebrows again. 'She's been bullying my sister …'

He looked at me carefully, and just nodded. 'Before or after?'

I looked confused. He said, 'Before or after you wrongly accused her?'

'Before *and* after, but it's in confidence because my sister didn't want me to tell you. She's embarrassed about it, and she's afraid telling will make it worse.'

He nodded grimly.

I said, 'well, umm, thanks...' and started to go, but he said, 'Denise?' so I stopped and looked at him.

'You're sure this is the truth?'

I looked amazed and outraged, so he explained, 'You're not just trying to get back at Jayne because she's the reason you were in trouble?'

My face cleared, 'God, no, *that's* all over,' I said airily.

It was too. It was nothing compared to our new crisis. He just nodded. He'd done a lot of nodding and eyebrow raising. This must be his 'hearing confidences' face.

So then I left to join Anna and Heeun setting up the stall.

Heeun said, 'Do you think he believed you? You didn't give any *proof.*' She looked worried. I looked worried too. Because I had a motive for making it up, that was the problem.

But Anna said, 'Nah, he'll do what he did to us... he'll check it out with someone else in their class, pretending that he knows *already*, and then he'll approach Jayne with a full case against her.'

That was cleverly worked out! And that's what he'd do, for sure. Those are just his sly tactics. (I must remember in the future if he tries them on me again!) So I relaxed. My job was over. I could enjoy the stalls and all. Not like poor Justine. She had to wait all day practically. And Heeun had to wait a few hours ...

We'd been collecting clothes for days so we had a good selection. We started hanging stuff on hangers. We had two plastic mannequins Anna had managed to borrow off Dunnes Stores!

She has loads of nerve, Anna, but also (she explained), if it's for charity, people always want to help you. Heeun started dressing the mannequins. We suspected she'd be the best stylist and sure enough, no sooner did she start matching stuff than it was bought. I was pretty jealous of this talent. She could take some old blue top and drape a scarf round it and it would suddenly look amazing. So our stall was going pretty well. There was a big crowd round it, and our cash till was going *ping! ping! ping!* and Anna was looking delighted. I think she loves the jangle of money even more than the sound of Jim Morrison's voice (allegedly her favourite sound).

Just as Heeun was re-dressing the mannequin, cause we'd just sold the dress off her, Declan came in with this girl in his class, Siobhan Reilly. I felt my face fall into impatient, haughty lines. I couldn't help it. That's just the expression my face assumes for Declan.

'Hey, guys,' he said, 'how you getting on?'

'Sold loads already,' said Anna cheerfully.

'That's Renata's, right?' said Siobhan Reilly, looking at the top Heeun was draping on the mannequin.

'Yes, how did you know?' said Heeun.

'I think I remember it on her last year ...' said Siobhan, 'but anyway, it kind of screams Renata, and given the connection ...' She smiled at Anna.

'Try it on,' said Declan.

Siobhan gave a loud laugh, very hearty, that went with her broad shoulders. 'It wouldn't even go over me.'

'Hmm, it's a bit ... flowery,' said Declan, frowning at it accusingly, 'but this ...' He took a khaki jacket off one of the hangers.

'Maybe,' said Siobhan. He helped her on with it, and patted it down on her shoulders. It was short on her but that didn't matter, it was aviator style.

'Nice,' said Heeun, moving in to zip it up.

'Hmm,' said Siobhan, admiring herself in the mirror, 'what do you think?' she turned to Declan.

'Yeah, looks great!' he said, reaching out to smooth her hair back behind her ears and turn her face to profile.

'If you don't buy it, I will,' said Anna, and she probably meant it. The jacket was just her style. But Siobhan bought it and walked off with Declan. He took her arm, hardly bothering to wave good bye to us. We looked after them.

'Whoa!' I said.

'Looks like he got lucky,' said Anna.

'She seems nice, I think,' said Heeun, 'and quite pretty in a tomboy-ish way.'

'Too good for him!' I said.

Anna started to laugh. 'But she's already making him look better, right? You're regretting it, right ...'

I pushed her. 'He never fancied me anyway,' I said, 'I always said he didn't and this proves it!'

'No, it doesn't. Just proves he got fed up of you doing the snotty face.' Then she did an imitation of my face looking at Declan – exaggerated, I hope, cause she looked like someone wrinkling her nose up against a bad smell.

I don't know did Declan fancy me ever. Possibly he is as pragmatic as Anna and was actually meeting hundreds of girls to help them with their blogs. I am glad I don't have to make that face at him any more, but I am sorry that the number of my admirers has gone down.

At half-eleven we closed the stall to go and watch the athletics championships. The whole school did. Anna had suggested a betting stall with odds on who'd win, but this wasn't allowed. It's okay to bet on the wheel of fortune, but not on one's fellow students apparently. Martha Connolly (from our class) was up for sprint *and* long jump, so we cheered like crazy but it went to Alison (in Third Year). When the races were over and everyone was moving back out to the stall, it was Heeun's big moment. Me and Anna watched (surreptitiously) as she went up to Justine and started chatting to her. They were deep in conversation (about the races presumably) and Heeun steered them (surreptitiously) towards Jayne O'Keeffe and her gang, and as they passed Heeun managed to simultaneously put out her foot *and* shove against Jayne so that she tripped right over and came down – *hard!* – on her knees. She looked up snarling. Her jeans were ripped at the knee and it was obvious they were her best jeans

cause everyone wears their best clothes in on the last day. Heeun was the picture of concern. We could see her, all fluttering hands and eyebrows – you'd have been insane to say she did it on purpose. But when she walked off with Justine, Jayne was gazing after them.

'Brilliant!' I hugged Heeun enthusiastically when she joined us back at the stall.

'Yes,' said Heeun modestly, 'it went good, and I think … the *right* level of injury. Her legs were scraped, but not broken.'

She sounded very scrupulous, as if she'd worked out exactly the amount of pressure that needed to be applied to the shove for *scraped, but not broken*. It was important to apply exactly the right pressure, because this was Jayne O'Keeffe's final punishment. I mean we weren't going to be tripping and shoving her every day, obviously. That would make *us* bullies.

'How did she take it?' said Anna, 'we couldn't hear.'

'Well,' said Heeun, 'I think she suspects, but can't prove. I said *oh sorry* sincerely, but then I said "It's awful to hurt people", emphasising *hurt* and then I took Justine's arm, so you know I think she knew … but anyway there's nothing she can do.'

No, nothing. That's why Heeun had to do it. If me or Anna had tripped up Jayne it would have looked deliberate. Too much history between us.

Anna said, 'The good thing is you look so sweet and non-violent, you can get away with loads.' She sounded pretty

jealous, as if she wanted to rework her own bolshy and aggressive image. People never think Anna's innocent.

The good clothes had all gone so the afternoon was gonna be hard work. You would have to be a genius salesperson to shift the tat we were left with – half the stuff was way old, like jeans with the bum rubbed right down (who gave *those*?) The other half was way out – an extraordinary purple and orange *tent* (well, dress). Heeun and Anna seemed to be relishing the challenge so I left them to it. Justine came on over, so they had her help.

Anyway, I thought it was my charitable duty to spend some money so I went to the wheel of fortune and staked on nine, my lucky number, and lost €3. Then I bought a hot-dog and smothered it with mustard and mayo and went over to check out the kissing stall. There was quite a commotion round it. I got there to see J.P. totally *songing* Celine and everyone whooping. It was quite something.

But then suddenly Mrs Moloney was at the front of the crowd and 'A quick peck is what I think we agreed,' she said quietly, not shouting, but everyone immediately stopped whooping and J.P. and Celine separated. 'Time up, I think Celine,' said Mrs Moloney and Celine looked kind of embarrassed and ran off. So the stall was empty. Joanne Dunne came over then, looking cross, and Mrs Moloney went over to have words with her.

'Oh God,' we heard Joanne say, 'bloody over-sexed second years! Sorry Mrs Moloney!' I looked at Elaine and giggled – *we*

weren't over-sexed. Then Mrs Moloney went off and Joanne looked harassed because Celine was supposed to do the full hour and now she'd no one to replace her.

'I need a volunteer!' she shouted.

Everyone just giggled and nobody was coming forward, but I'd an idea, so I raced back to our stall and said, 'Heeun! They need you at the kissing stall!'

Heeun said, 'What! No way Denise!'

I said, 'It's for charity! Go on! It's an emergency! Celine's been banned!'

'For what?'

'For songing J.P.!' – Anna and Heeun began to laugh – 'So you go, but just a peck, no getting carried away, now!'

'*You* go,' said Heeun, 'or Anna. *I'm* not.'

I said, '*You're* flavour of the month, you know you are, after your party.'

'Yeah, go on Heeun,' said Anna. We were all laughing, Justine too, and Heeun let herself be pulled away which I didn't think she would, but obviously the insane mood of the day was getting to her and she was still buzzed up from shoving Jayne.

We went up to Joanne, who said, 'Oh God, no! Not another over-sexed second year!' so Heeun looked highly offended.

'I am only here for charity!'

I said, 'Don't generalise! Celine is Celine, we're not all clones you know.'

So Heeun took her place and pretty soon Pierce came along sheepishly. I stayed to see what kind of kiss Heeun would give and sure enough it was the smallest butterfly flutter so Joanne looked relieved and I went back to take Heeun's place at the fashion stall.

Anna went off to get food and me and Justine tried to flog the clothes. But they were too hideous so after a bit we gave up and started competitions on who could make the mannequin look most foul. Justine got a long leopard-skin scarf and wrapped it around her head and I got a shaggy fake-fur coat, which looked like a dirty white carpet, and then Justine forced shiny gold leggings up her legs, and then we added a green leather bum-bag.

'Hey, actually she doesn't look too bad!' I said, 'in a kind of disco queen way…'

'Hmm,' said Justine, and added some sun-glasses, which totally worked, and then she began to laugh a bit manically, and took the red marker we were using to write prices and began *scrawling* on the fake-fur coat!

'Justine!' I howled. It was pretty anarchic. I remembered when we were small Justine was the one to carry things furthest in our games. She's actually quite nuts! I'd forgotten this when she went all quiet. She scrawled *Now I've got arms* right across the front and back of the coat. This was a pretty loopy, but inspired, thing to write. We stepped back.

'She looks amazing,' I said devoutly.

'She just needs gold boots,' said a voice behind us. We turned round. It was Derek.

'You like her?' I said.

'Yeah. Put her in the kissing stall,' said Derek, 'unless you'd like to go in yourself ...' and he gave me a cheeky smile. I blushed slightly, then laughed. I was surprised at Derek. This was a bold and daring thing to say, practically worthy of J.P.! 'Go on, it's for *charity*,' said Derek, and he winked at Justine and said, 'See you tonight, yeah?' and walked off, leaving me staring after until I pulled myself together to yell, 'I'm gonna be dressed like her!'

I have to admit I was glad Derek hadn't gone off with someone else like some other so-called admirers I could mention!

Then Justine started badgering me, 'Who's he? He's cool. Are you really gonna dress like that? You should! I think we've invented a brilliant new look.'

Then Anna and Heeun were back. They looked at the mannequin and folded their arms, and shook their heads disapprovingly, but couldn't keep from laughing.

'It's very fashion,' said Heeun earnestly, 'but it will only work on the cat-walk, I think. It is unwearable!'

'No, Denise is gonna wear it tonight to meet that boy with dark eyes,' said Justine.

'Oh, oh!' said Anna and Heeun, looking at me.

'How d'you get on?' I asked Heeun, quickly, to change the subject. 'Are you the most kissed?'

'I don't know,' she said modestly, 'but I did quite well. Lots of the boys from our class and some from the other years as well!'

'J.P?' I said curiously, 'David Leydon? Derek?'

'Not J.P. or *Derek*,' she said, giving me a sly look 'but David Leydon, yes.'

I absorbed this surprising piece of information. It was not at all the kind of thing I could imagine David Leydon doing. Maybe he fancied Heeun!

'Who replaced you?' I said.

'Nobody,' she said, 'I was time up …'

That reminded me! I checked my phone, 'Nearly time!' I said. We half swivelled our eyes to Justine. '*I'm* fine,' she said. But she'd definitely turned paler.

We began packing up the clothes. They weren't gonna sell in the ten minutes we'd left. Well, they weren't gonna sell in a *year*.

'Poor charity shops!' said Anna.

I saved the jacket – as a memento of Justine's craziness/creativity, not because I was going to wear it tonight. I was joking about that!

We ran off to assembly. We needed to get there early 'cause we needed to be in the front row. People were already there so we had to shove a bit to get to the front. There was Tommy and his band setting up. He winked at us. I felt gruesome. I looked at Justine and Heeun and Anna. They all looked gruesome.

Tommy's show was really the highlight of the day. It was €5

in. Practically the whole school was crowded into the assembly hall because everyone wanted to hear Jamón Jamón; that's the name of Tommy's band (it's pronounced 'Hamown Hamown' and it means 'ham ham' in Spanish). They're really good. Well we think so. They're smart too. They play some of their own stuff (so-so) and some Really Famous Stuff (brilliant, obviously). They kind of lull you into listening to their so-so stuff by rewarding you with Old Favourites. Like they kicked off with 'Common People', which everybody loves. How could you *not* love it? I practically forgot my fear I loved it so much. The hall went mad! And they were off, playing one of their own for every two famous ones. And some of their own were actually okay. They had a new one which had a pretty catchy tune and a chorus which by the end we were all singing along to.

And then Tommy announced, 'And now, for my Johnny Cash numbers, I need a June Carter' and he looked over the hall, up and down and round, till his eyes fell on Justine as if by chance and he pulled her up onto the stage!

She looked tiny and cute up there, in her jeans and stripey top.

I closed my eyes in sheer horror. My heart was going *thud-thud-thud*. It seemed to me that the whole hall had fallen silent with amazement.

And then: 'Now I've got arms,' sang Tommy, in his kind of throbbing, deep voice.

'And you've got arms,' came back an incredibly sweet, girlish voice.

I opened my eyes. That was Justine! She was holding a mike, looking just a tiny bit nervous, but no nerves in her voice.

'Let's get together and use those arms … Time's a wasting!' They both sang, perfectly in tune, gazing full at each other. They looked like they were in love! Justine didn't even look nervous any more. It was just incredible! I looked at Anna. Her mouth was popped open. She widened her eyes at me. We'd never imagined this!

They were singing Johnny Cash, which I recognised because Tommy is always listening to him. Probably a lot of people didn't know this particular song, it's not too famous, but it didn't matter, their voices sounded so good together.

As soon as they'd finished, Tommy and Justine launched without pausing into another Johnny Cash song, and it was a really funny one. It allowed them to show the difference between their voices.

'Daddy sang bass,' sang Tommy, pushing his voice real low.

'Mama sang tenor,' sang Justine, real high.

'Me and little brother would join right in there, in the sky, Lord, in the sky,' they both sang. Their voices really were brilliant together.

At the end there was an *avalanche* of applause. Tommy took Justine's hand and 'Justine Nelson!' he said into his mike (more clapping) and she smiled and waved like a real star and then he lowered her back down to the hall beside us, and he and his band started one of their own (so-so) songs. Unbelievable!

The rest of the concert passed in a delirium. I could not believe Justine had done that well. Of course she and Tommy had been practising for the past ten days, but even so ...! I never thought their voices would sound so *matched* and I never ever believed she could look that confident and sassy.

And I knew that that was the end of the bullying – we didn't even need O'Toole's intervention (though I was glad Jayne O'Keeffe was gonna get it from him). I knew it was the end of the bullying because even *I* was looking at Justine with completely new eyes. Like I've admitted here, I did think Justine was a bit annoying, but now I knew that every time I saw her I'd remember her up on that stage. Respect.

It was a pity Mum and Dad hadn't seen her.

Tommy's last number was a total anthem, so the hall went crazy. Then as we began to file out people started coming up to Justine, people from older classes, teachers even and 'you were amazing!' they were saying. Off-stage she'd gone back to being shy, so she just blushed and nodded but looked thrilled.

I think maybe she is now a celeb like Tommy. God! How am I going to handle this? I meant to *help* her, not to *promote* her.

Next I know J.P. will want to *song* her!

I had better ask Anna's mum how to handle these (perhaps inevitable) Feelings of Envy and Dissatisfaction.

But I was delighted when Justine told mum all about it. She gave me full credit for coming up with the idea, which I didn't

really (Anna did). I looked modest and sisterly. Mum was thrilled. She hugged us and said she was proud of us both. I think she meant it. I guess if you are a mum you are as proud of your daughter for being a boring thing like kind-hearted, as for being an exciting thing, like a singer.

The Most Momentous Day of Term, maybe of The Year, maybe of Our Lives (to date!) – wasn't even over yet. There is a postscript which I will write later, or maybe tomorrow or maybe the next day, because I am about to pass out from the effort and concentration involved in all this writing. And I need to wrap my presents …

FRiDAY DECEMBER 25TH

Christmas Day!

I am so bloated by food and drink – two glasses of champagne! – I really can't write. But I summoned up enough energy to write in the blog, because it would be very wrong not to wish happy Christmas to our loyal and faithful readers, so here's what I wrote, and it will have to do for this diary too:

Posted up on blog at 19:43

Happy Christmas everyone!
I have eaten: breakfast: croissants (2),
glass of orange juice with (small) glass of
champagne (this is called Buck's Fizz).
Dinner: turkey (2 slices breast, half leg),

stuffing, roast potatoes, more stuffing, cranberry sauce, brussels sprouts (two, had to force them down), more stuffing, salad, ham (two slices), more stuffing, pudding, champagne (1 glass), marzipan, chocolates …

So you see, am bloated with food and drink and it is a wonder I have enough energy to type, and please do not expect me to write anything witty!

This morning we went to the soup kitchen – me, and Hefto, and my little sister.

It was a special Christmas soup kitchen. The shops gave us loads of delicious food. There was turkey and stuffing and pudding, the full Christmas dinner. There was not so much chopping. No carrots! (Lucky homeless and lucky me!). I just had to top and tail Brussels sprouts (not so lucky homeless, and not so lucky me!), and peel potatoes.

A choir came in to sing. My little sister joined the choir and got to sing one verse of *Silent Night* all on her own because she was the smallest person there, and because she sings like an angel, and everyone said, *aaahhh* ….

As presents I got: from Santa: sparkly hair clips, leggings, mini-dress (Topshop), book (*The Diary of Anne Frank*)

From my sister: CD of Christmas carols [very cute present! Singing reminds me of her.]

From my parents: An iPod!

From Hefto: t-shirt (Topshop) with silhouette of face probably belonging to a Famous Icon From the Past (no! Not Marilyn Monroe! Someone Else). Gorgeous, but embarrassing! Did not get her anything! Forgot to tell her mine and Bomb's pact - we never buy each other Christmas presents, Bomb initiated this because she has so many brothers and sisters, if she had to get me something too she would run out of a) money and b) time.

Posted up on blog at 19:55

Xenawarrior cleaner

So you're stuffed then?

Posted up on blog at 20:38

Hefto's post:

Demise, do not worry, I did not expect a present from you! I just felt like getting you something. I hope this is not embarrassing you!

Happy Christmas all you people out there. We are not having Turkey and stuffing (what is stuffing???) We are having curry ...

Posted up on blog at 21:12

ZeeZee:

Do you guys ever think of *anything* but

songing and stuffing? (but happy Christmas anyway).

Posted up on blog at 22:10

Demise's post:

Sigh! Since you ask, on Friday we got one over the Bullies. But I don't like to big up my charity work …

Posted up on blog at 22:42

Bomb's post:

From my sister: book [*The Master and Margherita*, by Bulgakov]

From my eldest brother: poster [from the Soviet Union! Red, white and black! Very Cool!]

From my second brother: A Zippo lighter [second-hand but really cool! It is not for me to light cigarettes, he says, it is for making a fire if I get stuck overnight in a wood (as you do…)]

From my parents: bike [but great bike, free-estyle, i.e. no brakes, just back-peddle brakes, very streamlined frame.]

From Hefto: t-shirt (thanks Hefto!).

SATURDAY 26TH DECEMBER

Posted on blog at 13:14:

Happy Stephen's Day!

Still eating: sandwiches made with ham and turkey and stuffing, cold roast potatoes, marzipan crumbs... listening to Amy Whitehouse on iPod (latest song is frankly so-so!) and reading *Diary of Anne Frank* (good!)

Posted on blog at 13:18

Pippa:

Still with the stuffing?

Posted on blog at 13:53

CuriousinDenver:

What is this Stephen's Day? - Boxing Day, surely?

Posted on blog at 14:13

Bomb's post:

We say Stephen's Day ...

Gonna test my bike by freewheelin' to your house, Demise

SUNDAY 27TH DECEMBER

OK. The stuffing's all gone! Food and present interlude over! I will not make you wait the twelve days of Christmas to find out

how The Most Momentous Day of Term ended ...

So last Friday after The Triumph of All our Plans and The Routing of the Bullies we were going to Wesley, which is a disco which Keith goes to. He wanted Anna to come and she wanted us to come, and because it was the last day of term I was allowed. And obviously Keith's friend, David Leydon was there, and he brought his friends, Derek and Brian. So ...

You've guessed. Something has definitely got into Derek, I don't know what, maybe he got lessons from J.P., because he wasn't looking at me with quite that shiny, hopeful, enthusiastic look. He looked more cheeky.

Soon as he saw me, he said, 'Hey, you said you'd be wearing leopard-skin and fake-fur ...'

I said, 'That only works on the catwalk. It's unwearable, unfortunately.'

He said, 'But you saved the jacket? It was genius.'

Then he sang, '*Now I've got arms ...*' and kind of grabbed my shoulders, so I sang back at him (but not as well as Justine). And that was it, really. I mean that was me agreeing to his game. So when later he said did I want to dance, I said yes and I knew what I was saying yes to. So ...

First I couldn't think where to put my arms – round his neck, or round his waist? (Yes, let's get together, but how exactly do we use those arms?) There should be lessons in this. But I remembered it was called *necking*, for a reason I guess, so I put them

round his neck, and he grabbed me round the waist. It was not so frantic a kiss as my first Irish College kiss. It was more promising – a little bit enthusiastic and hopeful, but also a little bit cheeky. We crushed against the wall like the other couples for two whole songs (ha! another good reason for calling it *songing* – cause you do it to songs). When we stopped, I wasn't quite sure what to do. I mean it's pretty hard to just start talking about the music or something after that. There should be lessons in this too. We smiled a bit uncertainly at each other and wandered off to find the others.

He tried to hold my hand, and I fluttered it away from him because he isn't my boyfriend and I don't know if I want him to be my boyfriend, but he didn't put up with that, he reached for my hand again, and I moved away again, so then he said menacingly, 'Well, I've got arms' and put an arm around me, so I said 'And *I've* got arms' and knocked his arm off me. I can see we're going to be using our arms a lot to make jokes to push away the embarrassment!

Then he said, 'Dave fancies your friend Heeun.'

I said, 'Oh' and thought about this. There was no explosion of jealousy. So obviously I never actually fancied David Leydon. Not really fancied. Not like J.P. 'Well, he should tell her so,' I said impatiently.

'He wants me to tell you to tell her,' said Derek.

'Well that's *lame*,' I said, 'but sure, whatever.' I sounded kind

of annoyed. Maybe I did fancy David Leydon? But I think it's more that I was unimpressed by his cowardly tactics. I think I wanted him to be stronger and cooler and more confident than he actually is.

Anyway I did tell Heeun and she just giggled. She didn't song anyone although I think she was asked to dance (a.k.a., to song) a lot. I think she is gonna be like me (well like I *was*), way choosy (actually, I have to admit, she has more to be choosy about then I ever did, which is lucky for her. Because frankly there's no point being choosy, unless you've got lots to be choosy about. Otherwise it's not choosy, it's rejected).

Keith is still Anna's boyfriend. For the moment.

MONDAY 28TH DECEMBER

Wrote up our last day of school on the blog:

Okay people, Christmas stuffing over. Wanna hear about our last day at school? It was Charity Day. We raised €110 for charity at our stall. Our stall was a fashion stall. We took old clothes and sold them on.

Some people have a strange idea of what is acceptable to sell on. Jeans rubbed down to the bum anyone?

Another stall was the kissing stall. You paid to kiss whoever was in it. Hefto went in. She

got loads of paying kissers. (Just a peck, not *songing*).

Later that night at a disco Demise kissed (songed!) for FREE. Charity did not benefit. She is so selfish!

But the most important thing we did is: vanquished bullies by a three-pronged attack. We cannot say more in case someone from our school reads this. But here is our advice: when vanquishing bullies you must a) inform authority, b) wreak private vengeance [i.e. injure the bully in some way, but make sure you don't get caught!] and c) big up the victim [i.e. improve their self-confidence by concentrating on what they do really really well].

This approach will certainly work. From us to you, for free: Beating the Bully™.

TUESDAY DECEMBER 29TH

Oh whoa! Jesus! Well ...!

At Anna's today we went up to the computer to log onto the blog to read our comments. Well, there were the usual:

ZeeZee:

Glad you've found a way to bring your two obsessions, songing and charity together, but girls, I don't think charity demands *that* of

you

CuriousinDenver:

Thanks for the Christmas present, girls. Looking forward to Beating the Bully™ – have you patented it?

And a few more messages like that, just the usual. But then there was *this:*

DriftinginDublin:

Bomb, Demise and Hefto, you don't specify but I guess you live in Ireland – you left clues – Stephen's Day, Taoiseach – and I'm guessing it's Dublin … well I live there too! So let's meet up!

'Anna!' I squealed.

It was incredible, weird, just plain *bizarre* reading that. Our readers seem so far away, so remote, little words on a screen. And now … it was like a hand – a real, fleshy hand – had reached out from the screen and grabbed us. Or like one of our toys stood up and started talking. Or like a character in a book walked out from the pages and addressed us.

Truth is we didn't really think Xena or ZeeZee or curiousinDenver or any of them was actually *real.* Not a person you could *meet.*

But once I'd absorbed the shock I thought, *well yeah, it could be fun to meet driftinginDublin.*

'Where will we meet? In the shopping centre?' I giggled.

But Anna was looking way serious, very, very serious, 'Denise,' she said, 'what happens if he's … forty!'

'Forty!' I said, 'why would he want to meet us if he's *forty*. He knows we're at school …'

Then I stopped, appalled. My mouth hung open. I was remembering those articles I've read. This is exactly how dodgy forty-year-olds *do* meet school girls. Through the internet! This was terrifying! It wasn't just a hand reaching out to us. It was a *criminal* hand.

'Who says it's a *he*?' I said finally.

'We don't know,' said Anna, 'that's the point, isn't it? We just don't *know*.'

'We could ask him … *her*,' I said.

'Like he's gonna tell the truth,' said Anna impatiently.

'But maybe it *is* a school girl. Or a school guy,' I said longingly, 'he might be amazing.'

'Oh for God's sake!' said Anna.

'We'd have to get our parents to come to the meeting,' I admitted, 'or Renata!' I preferred that idea. Renata wouldn't compromise our street cred as much as parents.

'Like she'd bother,' said Anna, 'this is *Renata* you're talking about. Did you have her confused with Meg from *Little Women*?'

I giggled.

'But you're right about the parents,' said Anna. 'We'd better tell them now.'

'*Tell* them … *now!*' I said.

'Denise,' said Anna, 'If it is a … lepidopterist who's trying to catch a school girl to pin her to a slide, he has to be stopped.'

'A lepidopterist!' I shouted, 'A lecherous lepidopterist!'

So *that* was the hand coming out from the screen. A hand with a net trying to catch butterflies …

'Oh my God! Warn Heeun!' I cried hysterically.

'Calm down!' said Anna, 'He doesn't even know where we live yet.'

So we went downstairs to her kitchen, where actually *everyone* was. The whole family. Because her Dad was on holidays.

So we explained and then everyone trooped up to have a look at the blog. They read bits out. Which was mortifying! We should have censored first! Luckily nobody actually read out the bit about Heeun's party and Anna switching boyfriends.

'Jesus Christ!' said Renata, 'What fresh hell is this? You're not just lurching from crisis to crisis like the government … you're Zimbabwe – a total *illegal* mess.'

We waited. 'Oh, Renata!' said her mother, but good-natured. It seemed like she could hardly keep from laughing. Everyone kept reading out bits from the blog and laughing. It was mortifying! I wished we hadn't told them.

But then Anna's dad said heavily, 'I am not happy about men, or even boys, sitting in bedsits, sweating over my daughter's accounts of kissing.'

We gulped and the mood changed.

Anna's mum said, yes, it was ill-advised to communicate with total strangers without your parents' knowledge, and there was a reason Facebook protects your profile so that only approved people can read it etc. She said of course we imagined our readers were our own age and probably lots of them were, but we'd no way of knowing, that was problem. Then everyone discussed, like we weren't there, what we should do about it.

Renata said we'd created a Greek chorus and it was genius and we should just keep going! (Anna smirked at me then, really proud).

And their mum said yes, it was an impressive narrative, and maybe if we kept the parents in the loop … but their dad said it was a frivolous waste of time and a potential risk.

In the middle of all the arguing, I just looked at Anna and she nodded and we said, 'It's fine, we'll close it down,' and then we put on the faces of long-suffering martyrs, although actually I knew we were both looking for an excuse to shut it down.

How will our readers cope? I feel bad about them, but I also feel released. It was a burden having to meet those expectations every day.

WEDNESDAY 30TH DECEMBER

Went round to Heeun's. We told her the sad news of the blog. She said, 'Oh no! Awful! It will be *ishikoro*.'

'What's "*ishikoro*"?' we asked.

'It's a Japanese word for abandoned blogs,' said Heeun. 'It means "pebbles". You know like pebbles you pick up by the sea and then chuck away. Japan is full of abandoned blogs. It has thousands and thousands of *ishikoro*!'

We contemplated all these blogs chucked by the wayside. It made me feel very sad, and more guilty than ever over our poor little blog.

'What happens to them?' I asked.

'I think they just drift in cyberspace,' said Heeun.

Horrible! Even Anna was looking a bit choked up at the thought of our poor little *ishikoro* drifting round cyberspace for ever.

'We'd better explain,' I said heavily. We needed to post one last time to say goodbye and thanks to our readers.

Actually of course they were one step ahead of us.

CuriousinDenver:

Bomb, Demise and Hefto! You do know it's very unwise to meet strangers who contact you through the internet. drifitinginDublin, who ARE you? Why don't you tell the girls which school you're in? Your name? And gender?

'Good old CuriousinDenver' I said. 'Who needs parents or the police?'

We wrote:

This will be our last entry   ever. Our

parents are thinking like curiousinDenver.
Maybe driftinginDublin is a lecherous lepidopterist! So we have to stop writing and this
poor little blog is gonna be an ishikoro floating in cyberspace forever, which makes us very
SAD. But thank you for reading and commenting.
You were a lot of fun and a bit of help. Maybe
we will all be in touch again in four years time
when we are over eighteen and can do what we
like. Much love, xxx Bomb, Demise, and Hefto
p.s. if you do prescriptive texting, you might
find out our real names. p.p.s Happy New Year!

THURSDAY 31ST DECEMBER

Keith has invited us to his New Year's Eve party. So I will see Derek,
and Heeun will see David Leydon, and let's see what happens!

Our parents are so relieved that we're meeting boys our own
age that they're letting us stay till half one in the morning to see
in the New Year! We're not going to the party till 10pm anyway.
We are having a New Year's Eve dinner at home in my house
first. Anna and Heeun are coming.

Everyone is making resolutions because of how the year's
changing. For instance Justine is resolving to sing with Tommy's
band and make more friends, and my mum is resolving to do
more fun family things at the weekend, and Renata is resolving
to win the Booker Prize or something, but if you remember,

Anna and I don't do New Year Resolutions, we only do New *Term* Resolutions ... and I am getting a bit scared of these resolutions because my last New Term Resolution: 'do some exciting stuff to put on our blog' turned out a little *too* well. Like, if we hadn't been so desperate for adventures and a blog, we wouldn't have gotten into all this trouble. And in fact the best things that happened this term – getting friends with Heeun and with Justine – weren't planned. I never put down a resolution: Make Another Friend / Be Nice to Sister. I didn't even have a resolution: Song A Guy (I should have!). But all these things happened ... so this term I'm making no resolutions, and let's see how it turns out.

It might turn out a lot quieter. That's what they said in Anna's kitchen.

Her mum said, 'Well, you've had a very busy, emotional term, so I think this one will be calmer. That's the way things go.'

Her dad nodded, 'Boom and bust cycle.'

Renata said, 'But you're assuming they're subject to the usual laws ... Well, *I* think they're unstable gases. So they'll probably spontaneously combust this term.'

We waited – 'Oh, Renata!'

But the thing is Renata has a way of being right ... So is that what's going to happen next term? The Spontaneous Combustion Diaries? How will they compare to the Bad Karma Diaries ...?